HARD QUESTION

"So this is the feller everyone jabbers about," said the massive bruiser called Clem to his savage side-kick, Hiram. "The highfalutin Trailsman." He grinned, holding Skye down beneath his huge weight. "Downright puny if you ask me."

"This joker ain't no tougher than my nephew—and he's in diapers," Hiram agreed, showing his broken, jagged teeth.

"Well, let's earn our pay," Clem said, cocking an arm the size of a tree trunk. "Any last words, Trailsman?"

"I do have a question," Fargo said.

"A question?" Clem repeated. Sneering, he said, "Go ahead, puny feller. What you want to know?"

"You ever plan on having kids?" Fargo asked, and as he uttered the last word, his right knee drove up and in, slamming into the man-mountain's groin, driving so far in, Skye could have sworn it brushed the bruiser's spine.

Clem was waking up to the fact that the Trailsman was more than a legend—waking up with a scream. . . .

BE SURE TO READ THE OTHER THRILLING NOVELS IN THE EXCITING *TRAILSMAN* SERIES!

THE

TRAILSMAN

#189

MISSOURI MASSACRE

by

Jon Sharpe

A SIGNET BOOK

SIGNET
Published by the Penguin Group
Penguin Putnam Inc., 375 Hudson Street,
New York, New York 10014, U.S.A.
Penguin Books Ltd, 27 Wrights Lane,
London W8 5TZ, England
Penguin Books Australia Ltd,
Ringwood, Victoria, Australia
Penguin Books Canada Ltd, 10 Alcorn Avenue,
Toronto, Ontario, Canada M4V 3B2
Penguin Books (N.Z.) Ltd, 182–190 Wairau Road,
Auckland 10, New Zealand

Penguin Books Ltd, Registered Offices:
Harmondsworth, Middlesex, England

First published by Signet, an imprint of Dutton Signet,
a member of Penguin Putnam Inc.

First Printing, September, 1997
10 9 8 7 6 5 4 3 2 1

 REGISTERED TRADEMARK—MARCA REGISTRADA

Printed in the United States of America

The Trailsman

Beginnings . . . they bend the tree and they mark the man. Skye Fargo was born when he was eighteen. Terror was his midwife, vengeance his first cry. Killing spawned Skye Fargo, ruthless, cold-blooded murder. Out of the acrid smoke of gunpowder still hanging in the air, he rose, cried out a promise never forgotten.

The Trailsman they began to call him all across the West: searcher, scout, hunter, the man who could see where others only looked, his skills for hire but not his soul, the man who lived each day to the fullest, yet trailed each tomorrow. Skye Fargo, the Trailsman, and the seeker who could take the wildness of a land and the wanting of a woman and make them his own.

*1861—Missouri, the Show-Me State,
where those who let their guard down
are quickly shown how deadly
the frontier can be . . .*

1

The anguished squeal of a horse in agony jarred Skye Fargo awake.

For most of that morning the Trailsman had been slowly winding his way westward along a rutted road that paralleled the Missouri River. The thick muggy air, the buzzing drone of insects, and the gentle gurgle of the broad river had combined to make his eyelids as heavy as lead. Halfway between St. Louis and Jefferson City, he had taken to dozing in the saddle. He knew it was dangerous, but he could not help himself.

Dangerous, because war was brewing. Several Southern states were on the verge of seceding from the Union. The issue of slavery was doing what the British and the rest of America's enemies had never been able to do. It was tearing the country apart.

Many feared that if Abraham Lincoln was to be elected president in the fall, war would break out.

Already, rival factions were often at each others' throats. Groups of armed men roamed at will. Homes were burned. Partisans on both sides had been brutally shot or hung.

To make matters worse, outlaw bands were taking advantage of the turmoil to plunder and rape and murder as they saw fit. Missouri was one of the states hardest hit by the violence.

It had become so bad that lone travelers took their lives in their hands. Going about after dark was discouraged. When men went anywhere, they went armed. And they regarded anyone they did not know with suspicion.

Fargo had never seen the like. A dozen times that morning he had come on fellow wayfarers. All of them had given him a wide berth while nervously fingering rifles or revolvers. Once a family in an open wagon had clattered past, heading east. Fargo had smiled and touched his hat brim. In response, the brawny farmer holding the reins had dropped a hand to a shotgun resting across his lap. The threat had been as plain as the farmer's scowl.

It was a shame, Fargo mused. The people of Missouri had always been so friendly, so kind.

The big man in buckskins was glad that in a few days he would reach Kansas City. There, he would treat himself to a couple of nights spent gambling in the company of a certain lusty dove he was fond of. Then he planned to strike off across the vast prairie to the Rockies.

Fargo had earned some time to himself. He had just delivered an urgent Army dispatch from Denver to St. Louis in record time. Days of grueling travel had left him exhausted from lack of sleep and gaunt from lack of food. His pinto stallion was no better off. The Ovaro plodded along with its head drooping, its tail limp.

That is, until those piercing whinnies rent the humid Missouri air. Both Fargo and his stallion were instantly alert.

Fargo's right hand automatically dropped to the Colt strapped to his right hip. His keen lake-blue eyes probed the road and the green wall of vegetation that bordered it. A woman's scream eclipsed the squeals, punctuated by the crack of a gunshot that goaded him into applying his spurs just lightly enough to bring the pinto to a gallop.

Fresh ruts of a distinctive size and depth gave Fargo a clue to the source of the whinnies. Around two bends he swept, reining up sharply as he went around the second. With good reason.

A stagecoach had come to an abrupt stop forty feet away. It had to, or else it would have crashed into a huge tree that lay sprawled across the road. As it was, the driver had not had enough time in which to react. He had tried to stop the team, but momentum had carried the foremost pair into the obstacle. One horse was down, thrashing in a frenzy. The other reared, kicking at a limb that gouged its belly.

All this Fargo took in at a glance. Of more immediate interest was the stage and those who ringed it.

Perched on the seat was the driver, frozen in place with a hand pressed to a bloody shoulder. On the dusty ground beside the front wheel lay the motionless guard, bright scarlet stains creeping across the front of his shirt.

Those responsible had the stage hemmed in on either side. Five scruffy men wearing bandannas over the lower halves of their faces, their hat brims pulled low, held leveled pistols.

A sixth gunman had dismounted and flung the door wide. He was gesturing for those inside to step out. An elderly woman appeared. Stepping back, he impatiently wagged his pistol. The terrified matron awkwardly climbed down and was roundly cursed for being so slow.

So far Fargo was in luck. The racket the team was making had drowned out the thud of the Ovaro's hooves. And since he had halted before he was fully in the open, the bandits were unaware of his presence. He palmed his Colt, but did not shoot. Not when the elderly woman might be caught by stray lead.

"Come on, damn your mangy hides!" the impatient gunman rasped. "We don't have all day!" He was a tall drink of water, his chin covered with stubble, a thick mustache framing his upper lip. His filthy clothes, a red flannel shirt, overalls, and a battered brown hat, were fit to be burned.

Next to emerge was a mouse of a man in a gray suit and bowler, a black valise clutched to his chest as if it contained precious gems. "What is the meaning of this outrage, sir?" he demanded in a mousey voice that perfectly matched his mousey features.

"Can't you guess, idiot?" growled the gunman. Grasping the front of the passenger's shirt, he yanked.

The mouse squeaked in fright as he was flung to the earth with such force he lost both the bowler and the black bag. To his credit, he was more mad than afraid, and he pushed up off the dirt, sputtering in fury. "How dare you! No one manhandles Mortimer J. Forbush! I'm a lawyer, and I'll see you thrown into prison until you rot!"

A couple of the mounted bandits cackled. One nodded at their apparent leader and said, "Better watch yourself, hoss! That law wrangler is liable to bust your skull with one of those thick law books his kind tote everywhere!"

Their leader was not amused. Without warning, he kicked Forbush in the stomach, then snarled, "You have a leaky mouth, pilgrim." Bending, he snatched up the valise. "What's in this bag of yours, that you were hugging it to death? Money, maybe?"

"No! Don't!" Mortimer yelled, but he was in too much pain to prevent the outlaw from opening the valise and dumping the contents. A folder and dozens of sheets of paper fluttered to the ground. "Those are important documents!"

"Are they, now?" the gunman sneered. Hiking a boot, he was going to stomp on the pile when he realized another passenger was climbing down.

"Leave him be, you mean man!"

A pint-sized wildcat tore into the leader, flailing at him with tiny fists and feet. It was a girl of ten or twelve, as fearless as she was rash. Her attack took the gunman and his companions by surprise. Stupefied, they gawked, then burst into rowdy mirth. Except for their leader. He gripped the girl's wrist and shook her as a coyote might shake a marmot it was about to devour.

"That's enough out of you, sprout! Behave or I'll turn you over my knee!" So saying, the gunman flung her down next to the lawyer. But she bounced right back up and would have torn into him again had Mortimer J. Forbush not snagged her ankle.

"My ma used to say that only yellow dogs pick on women and kids! What does that make you, mister?"

A bearded bear on a roan slapped his thigh and hollered, "She sure is a hellion, Krill. Careful, or she might whup you!"

The leader stiffened and glared. So did some of the other outlaws. The bear on the roan, suddenly aware of his mistake, flushed and declared, "Damnation! Me and my big mouth. Now what do we do?"

"What do you think, stupid?" Krill shot back.

"But she's so young and pretty," the bear said sullenly. "It goes against my grain to make wolf meat of children."

Krill had a sharp retort on the tip of his tongue, but just then another figure stepped from the stage, and he spun, raising his six-gun. His open mouth yawned wider, as did his eyes. All the cutthroats, in fact, were so dazzled by the figure that they gaped in brutish amazement tinged with rising lust.

Fargo had seen the woman before they did. She was dressed in a fine, full dress that could not conceal the shapely swell of her bosom or the tantalizing curve of her slender hips and legs. Burnished brown hair was held up in a fashionable bun, revealing a smooth neck and rounded shoulders. Her face was exquisite. Cherry lips curled in defiance. Blue eyes blazed disdain. Her nose would have done justice to a statue sculpted by a master sculptor. High cheeks and a square chin hinted at inner strength.

"You will not lay a finger on that girl, or on any of us," the vision of loveliness stated. Moving to the child's side, she draped a protective arm over the girl's shoulders. "Rob us and go, Bart Krill."

The leader was taken aback by her defiance. "How do you know who I am?" he blurted.

The woman sniffed. "Oh, come now. Everyone in these parts has heard of you. For four years you have preyed on innocents like ourselves. You've stopped stages, waylaid merchants, even attacked settlers in their houses." Her chin jutted forward. "You are vermin, Bart Krill. As vile as any man who ever drew breath."

More laughter rumbled from the bear on the roan. He found humor in everything, it seemed. "Hear that, Krill?" he taunted. "You're so famous, we might as well not bother covering our faces anymore."

"Shut up, Barstow!" Krill fumed. Jabbing his revolver at the beauty, he snarled, "Since you know so much about me, Miss-High-And-Mighty, you know what to expect before we're through, don't you?"

At that the woman blanched and firmed her grip on the child. The lawyer had risen to his knees and was collecting his documents. Raw terror riveted the elderly woman where she had stopped.

Fargo cocked his Colt. He was anxious to do something, but any move he made would put the lives of the passengers in peril. If only the gunmen would lower their pistols! He saw Krill stalk to the stage and glower at the driver.

"Throw down the box, and be quick about it!" The outlaw had the look of a rabid wolf about to pounce. It would not take much to set him off.

Meekly, the driver complied. A middle-aged man, he was smart enough not to do anything that would cause Krill's trigger finger to tighten. Grunting, he hoisted the heavy metal strongbox out of the front boot and onto the lip of the seat. Pausing to balance himself, he pushed, and the strongbox thudded at Krill's feet.

The outlaw turned the box over and swore bitterly at finding a padlock as big as his hand. "What the hell is this?" he demanded. "I've never seen one this size before."

"It's the owner's idea," the driver said. "To make it harder for anyone who has no business opening the box."

"Is that so?" Krill said angrily, and like a striking rattler he pivoted and put a slug in the driver's torso. At the blast, the elderly woman screamed. The driver's hand flew to his sternum. He tried to speak but failed, then he pitched from the seat to wind up in a disjointed heap next to the express guard.

"You beast!" cried the woman who was shielding the girl. "I hope they catch you and hang you for this!"

Krill turned and leered at her. "If they do, you won't be around to see it, bitch." Motioning at two of his men, he barked, "Get off those nags and unhitch the team. I want the strongbox tied onto one of the horses. We'll open it later, once we're in the clear."

As the pair swung down, Fargo edged the Ovaro forward. He was upset with himself. Had he acted sooner, the driver would still be alive. The passengers would soon share the poor man's fate unless he did something right away.

Bart Krill faced them. Hitching at his belt, he swaggered toward the woman, his features a wicked mask of sadistic evil. "What's your name, sister?"

"Why do you want to know?" she said.

Again Krill struck, this time lashing out with the back of a hand that caught the woman full on the cheek and staggered her. The little girl leaped to the woman's defense, but she was swatted aside as casually as if she were a fly. She collided with the lawyer, who kept her from falling. The elderly matron recoiled in horror.

Fargo tensed. The pair unhitching the team had holstered their hardware. Barstow and the remaining two were watching Krill's antics. All but Barstow had lowered their pistols. He would never have a better chance.

"Bethany Cole, as if it's any of your business," the beauty revealed. She had no choice. Krill had elevated a fist to hit her again. "I teach school in Jefferson City. My brother is a deputy there. He will hunt you to the ends of the world if you so much as lay a finger on me."

Krill snickered. "Oh, I aim to do more than poke you with my *finger*," he gloated, and hungrily ogled her lush body. "So what if your kin is a lawdog? We've had more posses on our tail than a coon dog has fleas, and they ain't caught us yet. I reckon your brother won't be any luckier than they were." Brazenly, he extended a grimy hand toward her breasts. "Let's see if that's all you in there."

"Don't you dare!" Bethany cried, swatting his arm. "I'd rather die than let you have your way."

With a flick of both ankles, Skye Fargo spurred the stallion into a gallop and swept into the open. He banged a shot at one of the mounted outlaws who snapped in his direction. The man dropped like a stone. Immediately, Fargo aimed at Bart Krill, thinking he had the killer dead to rights, but Krill was craftier than he gave the man credit for being, and unbelievably fast. In a bound Krill reached the schoolmarm, clamped a forearm around her throat, and shoved her in front of him, using her as a living shield.

Fargo veered into the growth on the left side of the road as pistols cracked and lead buzzed around him. He answered, but did not score. A tree trunk he passed was smacked by a slug. The tip of a branch was clipped off above him. Reining up, he fired at one of the bandits who had been unhitching the team. The bullet caught the man in the leg just as he climbed onto his horse. Slumping over the saddle, the outlaw goaded the animal into racing off down the road.

Bart Krill was backing toward his own mount. Bethany Cole struggled mightily, but Krill's whipcord frame harbored sinews of steel. He reached his horse and paused to bellow, "The strongbox! Someone get the damn strongbox!"

But the rest of the hardcases were more interested in saving their own carcasses. The other man who had been working on the team was already astride a dun and racing pell-mell eastward. Another killer joined him. That left Barstow to cover Krill as the latter prepared to fork leather.

"Hurry up!" Barstow thundered, firing at random. "I can't see where the *hombre* went."

Krill cast a last, longing glance at the strongbox, then

shoved the teacher and vaulted onto his bay. "Bunch of cowards!" he raged.

Fargo wanted to stop the butcher at all costs. Streaking toward the road, he squeezed off a shot at the very split second that Krill wheeled the bay. His shot missed. Barstow came to Krill's aid, shooting twice. One of the leaden hornets clipped Fargo's hat. Bending low over the saddle, Fargo slanted to the right to put a thicket between them. When he straightened, Krill and the big bear were skirting the downed tree. Both sent lead into the vegetation to pin him down long enough for them to gain the straight stretch beyond.

Fargo raced in pursuit. Breaking from cover near the stagecoach, he reined toward the tree, only to be brought to a halt by a shout from Bethany Cole. "Stop! Please! Don't leave us!"

She had regained her feet. The elderly matron had broken into tears and was being comforted by the lawyer, while the little girl was staring in mute dismay at the body of the driver.

For a few moments Fargo wavered, torn between trying to bring an end to Krill's reign of terror and doing what he could for the passengers. It was the child who made up his mind for him. Running to the driver, she knelt and placed a hand on the man's forehead.

"Miss Cole! Mr. Forbush! Come here! I think Mr. Weaver is still alive!"

Reluctantly, Fargo watched the fleeing outlaws vanish around a bend. If the girl was right, going after them was out of the question. An innocent man's life was at stake. Jumping down, he dashed to the driver.

Weaver's eyes were open, mirroring great torment. Gasping in agony, he said, "I hurt! Oh God, how I hurt!"

"We have to get him to a doctor," Bethany Cole declared.

Which was easier said than done, Fargo mused. They could not go anywhere with that massive tree blocking the road. "Tend him as best you can," he told the schoolmarm, then hurried to the team. The stricken horse was back on its feet and acting none the worse for its ordeal.

After making sure the traces and harness on all six animals were secure, Fargo unhitched the team by separating the tongue from the coach. It took some doing, but he soon had them turned around. Now came the hard part. Using his lariat and a rope taken from the horse of the outlaw he had slain, he tied several loops around the maple and made the other ends fast to the wagon tongue.

Picking up the reins, Fargo let out with a whoop and flicked them at the horses. Automatically the team surged forward, but they were brought up short. Fargo urged them on, pitting their powerful bodies against the immense weight of the tree. Again and again he whipped the rear animals. Again and again the whole team threw itself into the effort.

At first nothing happened. Fargo was beginning to think the maple was too heavy. A grating sound convinced him to the contrary. Inch by gradual inch, the tree slid from its resting place, angling toward the south side of the road. By holding to the border and carefully gauging the angle, Fargo dragged the upper end far enough off the road to permit the stage to get by.

Undoing the ropes, Fargo turned the team a second time. Once he aligned the tongue with the rod shafts, it was a simple matter to reattach it. They were ready to go. Or almost. He tied the Ovaro to the rear, set his Henry up on the driver's seat, and replaced the strongbox in the front boot.

Weaver was unconscious but breathing. Bethany Cole held one of his callused hands, the little girl the other. She looked up at Fargo, revealing eyes the same color as his own.

"Stand back," Fargo directed. Stooping, he gently lifted the older man and eased Weaver onto the floor of the coach. A folded blanket on the right seat sufficed as a pillow. It was the best they could do under the circumstances.

"Climb in and hold on tight," he advised. "You're in for the ride of your lives."

They recognized the urgency. Even the child clambered swiftly back inside without comment, and Fargo slammed the door. As he placed a foot on the hub of the front wheel and reached up to grasp the rail that framed the driver's box, the lawyer stuck his head out the window.

"What about the holdup man you shot, stranger? And the express messenger? Surely we're not going to let them lie there for scavengers to eat?"

Fargo frowned. Leave it to a lawyer to nitpick when every moment they wasted was critical. "You can stay here until help comes, if you want, and shoo the buzzards and coyotes away."

"By *myself?*" Forbush said. "Why, Krill might return. Or wolves might show up. Or . . ."

"Figures," Fargo muttered and pulled himself up. In short order he leaned the Henry against his leg, worked the brake lever, hefted the whip a few times, and lumbered the team into motion with a sharp crack of the lash over their heads.

The Central Overland stage swayed as Fargo moved it into the middle of the road. He had handled Concords before, but never under these circumstances. Over eight feet high and weighing more than a ton, they had the ungainly aspect of overfed geese. Thanks to their ingenious design, though, which suspended the carriage on thoroughbraces made of three-inch-thick strips of leather, riding in one was like riding in a cradle on wheels. Sturdily built, they took any abuse.

Fargo proved that. He pushed the six horses to their limit, taking turns at breakneck speed. Several times the coach leaned so far to either side that the inner wheels spurned the ground. When the going was straight, he fairly flew, heedless of ruts, holes, and dips. The stage jounced and bounced and creaked and rattled. Twice the lawyer called out, upset, but Fargo ignored the protests.

Never for a moment did Fargo think of stopping to rest. He roared like a lion at anyone who blundered into his path. Some people shook their fists and hurled oaths, but he did not care.

In the middle of the hot afternoon the stage rumbled into Jefferson City. Fargo had been there before. So he had no trouble locating the Holladay Overland Mail Express Company. Bringing the sweat-lathered team to a halt right in front of it, he yelled, "The stage was held up! We need help!"

As usual, a crowd was on hand. They thronged around the Concord. Company officials whisked Weaver into the office and sent for a doctor and the town marshal.

In all the confusion and excitement, Fargo was largely forgotten. He walked to the rear boot, untied the Ovaro, and was about to slip quietly off when someone tugged on his elbow.

"Hold on there, stranger," Mortimer J. Forbush said. Beside him was the little girl. Behind him stood the schoolmarm and the matron. "None of us have thanked you properly for saving our lives."

"No need," Fargo said. He was tired and sore and hungry enough to eat a buffalo raw. A hot bath, a thick steak, and half a bottle of whiskey, and he would feel like a whole man again. Nodding at the ladies, he prepared to depart.

"What's your name, sir, if you don't mind my asking?" Bethany politely inquired.

"Skye Fargo, ma'am."

Suddenly, the lawyer became as rigid as a fireplace poker. "It can't be!" he exclaimed. "After all this time! To meet you like this!"

"What are you jabbering about?" Fargo asked, then saw the child. She wore a peculiar expression, and she gulped air as if she had something stuck in her throat. "Are you all right, little one?" he asked, perplexed.

Throwing her arms wide, the girl clasped his legs and

clung to him as if afraid he would try to run off. "We've found you! At long last!"

"What's this all about?" Fargo said. "Why are you acting this way?"

The girl pulled back. "Don't you know?" Her next words startled him to his core. "You're my *pa*!"

2

For all of ten seconds Skye Fargo was too dumfounded to
speak. His thoughts swirled in a jumbled vortex of doubt
and vague suspicions.

Could it be true? Fargo was the first to admit that he had
a special fondness for the fairer sex. It wasn't his fault that
he drew pretty females to him like a magnet drew iron
shavings. Women were fond of virile, handsome, vigorous
men—and he was more handsome and virile than most.

So it was no surprise that Fargo had never lacked for bed
partners. It was safe to say that he'd had more than what
might be called his "fair share." A close friend once joked
that if all the ladies Fargo had known were to lie down head
to toe in a straight line, they'd stretch clear from Denver to
China. The friend had been exaggerating, of course. But
Fargo could not deny that women were his abiding passion.

Quite naturally, as any man would, Fargo had sometimes
wondered if any of his dalliances resulted in an unforeseen
surprise later on. Since none of the women had ever con-
tacted him to that effect, he had taken it for granted that all
was well.

He would never admit as much to anyone, but he had
even begun to think that maybe, just maybe, he was one of
those who *couldn't* have kids.

Now this.

Fargo studied the little girl, noting again how her lake-
blue eyes were the spitting image of his. Her chin resembled his, too. But there any resemblance ended. Her cheeks,

22

her ears, the general shape of her face, they were all different. Which did not mean much. She might, after all, take more after her mother than she did her father.

The girl brought Fargo's reflection to an end by tugging on his pants and asking earnestly, "What's the matter? Aren't you glad to see me, Pa?"

"Quit calling me that," Fargo said a bit more irritably than he meant to, and promptly regretted it. Hurt, she jerked back as if he had slapped her. Lowering his voice, he said, "What makes you think that I'm your father, anyway? Who the blazes are you?"

"Amanda," the girl said nervously. "Amanda Templeton. Most folks just call me Mandy." She offered her hand for him to shake, but he hesitated, feeling awkward and uncertain. At that, the schoolmarm stepped up and jabbed an accusing finger.

"Well, I never!" Bethany Cole declared. "What sort of brute are you? After all this sweet child has just been through, you treat her like this? Have you no sense of decency?"

The elderly matron bobbed her chin in agreement. Her fiery stare indicated that she would like to see him banished to the infernal depths of Hell that very moment.

"Now hold on—" Fargo began, but he was cut off by the lawyer, who cleared his throat and spoke loud enough to be heard a block away.

"Now, now, Miss Cole. You're being unduly hard on this poor fellow. Until a moment ago, Mr. Fargo had no idea that he even had any offspring. Small wonder the shock has affected him as it has." He rested a hand on Fargo's arm. "Perhaps we should meet later to discuss the issue? I have a lot of important papers for you to sign."

The man's oily smile and false familiarity rankled Fargo. Shrugging the pale hand off, he snapped, "How the hell do you fit into this, mister?"

Bethany Cole blinked, then covered the child's ears.

"Really, sir! Watch your language in front of Mandy, if you please!"

"Don't you have a class to teach somewhere?" Fargo responded. The last thing he needed was a busybody poking her nose into his affairs. Her good looks aside, she was really beginning to annoy him.

"I'll have you know that school is out for the summer. I'm on vacation. My time is my own."

"Fine. Then why don't you spend it somewhere else? Go celebrate. The Cork and Crown has some of the best whiskey this side of the Mississippi, and it's just down the street."

The schoolmarm flushed, then flared with anger. "Are you suggesting that I go into a *tavern*? No decent woman would ever soil herself by hobnobbing with drunken riffraff."

Maybe it was her attitude. Maybe Fargo's rising resentment was to blame. Or maybe it was a combination of both that made him say without thinking, "I should have known. You're one of *those*."

"Those what?" Bethany challenged.

"Never mind." Fargo glanced at the girl again, who was regarding him with a mixture of fear and something else. Dislike? No. Peering deeper, he would have sworn that she found the whole situation highly hilarious. "Where's your mother? Why isn't she with you?"

Mortimer J. Forbush harrumped. "I will gladly answer all your questions, sir. But not here in the street. Perhaps you would see fit to repair to the lobby of the Hotel Excelsior, where we have reserved a room?"

"You still haven't told me what this has to do with you," Fargo curtly reminded him.

"I was retained by Amanda's mother to track you down," Mortimer said. "Beyond that, I will not say, not until we have some privacy."

Only then was Fargo aware that a number of passersby had stopped to eavesdrop. Whirling on them, he said in exasperation, "Don't you jackasses have better things to do?"

They slunk off, but they were not happy about being insulted, and when Fargo turned, he saw the matron departing in a righteous huff, as well. He never had learned her name. As for Bethany Cole, she was looking at him as if he were a loathsome insect she would like to crush underfoot. Mandy was trying to hide a grin.

"Do you agree?" Forbush prodded. "Should we adjourn to the hotel?"

"I'll be there in an hour," Fargo said.

The law wrangler puckered his brow. "Do you have any idea of the lengths I have gone to in my client's behalf to locate you? What could possibly be so important that we can't do it right this minute?"

"My horse," Fargo said and led the Ovaro off without another word. After the long, grueling race to reach Jefferson City, it needed to be watered, fed, and groomed.

The stallion always came first when Fargo hit a town. Like every other frontiersman, he depended on his mount for his very survival. There was a unique bond between them. They were linked in a way that an Easterner could never understand. He never thought of the stallion as his possession. The Ovaro was more akin to a four-legged friend.

At a stable on Baker Street Fargo boarded his friend for the night. He fed and curried it himself. As he stroked the currycomb, he racked his brain, peeling back the years to recall the women he had known ten years ago, or better. Was one of them Mandy's mother?

He had been so young then, still wet behind the ears. His memory of several ladies was vivid. Others were hazy. Either he had not known them long, or they had not made a deep impression.

True to his word, Fargo arrived at the hotel an hour later. Over his left shoulder were his saddlebags, in the crook of his right arm the Henry.

Seated in oak chairs in the lobby, waiting, were Mortimer J. Forbush, Amanda Templeton, and, to Fargo's mild surprise and annoyance, Bethany Cole. Deliberately, he walked past them to the desk and signed for a room, leaving his belongings with the desk clerk for the time being. He was stalling and knew it, but it could not be helped.

His gut twisted into a knot every time he considered that he might actually be the girl's father. What was he to do? What did her mother expect of him? He wasn't ready to settle down. The mere notion provoked a cold sweat. Had the odds at last caught up with him?

Mortimer had risen and was tapping his toe. "So glad you could make it," he said as Fargo came over. "I've taken the liberty of reserving a table in the dining room. We can talk while we eat if you don't mind."

Fargo pointed at the schoolmarm. "What's she doing here?"

"I can answer for myself," Bethany said testily and patted Mandy. "It has come to my attention that this poor child has been traipsing all over creation in search of you, with no one else for company other than Mr. Forbush. It isn't fitting that a young lady travel without a proper chaperone. So, until you do what honor requires, I have appointed myself as her temporary guardian."

Fargo could tell that the lawyer was not pleased by the development. The schoolmarm had a point, though, so all he said was, "Suit yourself. Just so you don't meddle."

"Perish forbid," Bethany said stiffly. "I won't say another word about your despicable behavior."

"Despicable?" Fargo said, spoiling for an argument, but the lawyer took Mandy's hand and guided them toward an arched doorway on the right.

The Hotel Excelsior was one of Jefferson City's finest. Its spacious, lavish dining room was frequented by the cream of the social crop. Men wore pressed suits and polished shoes. Women had on frilly dresses and sparkling jewelry. Some were fanning themselves.

Fargo became the focus of attention. In his buckskins and spurs, he stood out like the proverbial sore thumb. Several men gazed at him in open contempt. Several women graced him with friendly smiles.

The table was in a corner. Forbush seated Mandy and the schoolmarm, then started to sink into the chair that fronted the room.

"That one is mine," Fargo said.

"What difference does it make?" Mortimer asked.

"When you've made as many enemies as I have, you don't take chances," Fargo said, claiming the seat as his own. Although it was unlikely anyone in Jefferson City meant him harm, keeping his back to a wall was second nature.

Bethany Cole's full red lips quirked. "Do you mean to say there are people who don't like you? I can't imagine why."

Her sarcasm sliced into Fargo like a Bowie. "I thought you weren't going to say another word," he noted.

"Now, now," Mortimer said, as if chiding a pair of children. "Let's be civil, shall we? I only consented to having you join us, Miss Cole, for Amanda's sake. Please don't make me regret my decision."

Thankfully, the waiter came. After they ordered their food, he started to leave, but Fargo was not done. "Bring me a whiskey," he directed.

Bethany fidgeted. "Is that wise? What sort of example are you setting for your daughter?"

"Make it a bottle," Fargo amended, and out of the corner of his eye he observed Mandy cover her mouth and silently titter with glee. What was that all about?

"You're impossible, sir," the schoolmarm said.

"I'm a grown man, and I'll do as I damn well see fit," Fargo rejoined.

The lawyer sighed. "Is this what I must put up with all evening?" Shaking his head, he set his valise on the table and opened it. "Where should I begin?" he wondered aloud, then leaned toward Fargo. "Tell me. Were you, or were you not, in St. Louis ten years ago this month?"

Fargo had to think. He might have been. He had traveled a lot that year, on both sides of the Mississippi. Dimly, he seemed to recollect venturing there once, but only for a week or so, and in late fall, not late spring. "I might have been," he allowed.

"Do you happen to remember a woman called Rosalie Templeton? She is Amanda's mother."

The name did not jog Fargo's recollection any. He shook his head.

"Think carefully," the lawyer said. "She would have been eighteen years old then. Quite attractive, too, judging by how well she preserved her charms." Mortimer paused. "Imagine a woman about six feet tall with auburn hair and flashing blue eyes. She had a creamy complexion and a dimple on her chin. Does that jog your memory?"

For the life of him, Fargo could not recall a woman who fit that description. "No," he confessed.

Bethany Cole had been squirming as if she sat on hot coals. Now she exploded, saying, "What else did you expect, Mr. Forbush? It's obvious that he wants nothing to do with Mandy. He's not man enough to admit he's her father."

"Maybe I'm not," Fargo said. "Did you ever consider that?"

"Oh, please," Bethany responded. "Everyone else can see the resemblance. Why can't you?"

Fargo was saved from having to reply by the timely arrival of the waiter bearing his whiskey. Snatching the bottle from the silver tray, he dispensed with the glass. It seared his throat and mouth, burning warmth into his stomach, relaxing him enough so that he was not offended when the schoolmarm made another comment.

"Honestly, sir. Must you act like a barbarian in public? Guzzle your swill in your own room, rather than inflict your crude manners on the rest of us."

In response, Fargo looked her in the eyes and smacked

his lips. "It wouldn't hurt you to try some, lady. Might take that starch out of your collar."

"I am perfectly content with how I am, thank you."

"Do tell. And when was the last time you let your hair down and really enjoyed life? When was the last time you laughed so hard that your sides hurt? Or the last time you let a man so much as touch you?" Fargo was being rude, but he did not care. She had brought it on herself by treating him as if he were pond scum. Taking a healthy swig, he offered her the bottle. "Prove me wrong and I'll apologize."

Bethany Cole was a study in simmering indignation. She gripped the butter knife, and for a moment Fargo thought she was going to hurl herself at him. She had spunk, sure enough. Under her prim exterior lurked a tigress itching to bust out.

Forbush was peeved and it showed. "I refuse to conduct business with these constant distractions. Do we continue? Or must we meet again tomorrow?"

Fargo gestured for the lawyer to go on while treating himself to another generous swallow of coffin varnish. At a nearby table sat a plump woman wearing enough jewels to sink a canoe. Scorn etched her face, and it deepened when he winked at her and jiggled the bottle in invitation.

Someone laughed. Not the lawyer, and certainly not the schoolmarm. From little Mandy Templeton pealed hearty laughter that drew a glance of reproach from Forbush and of shock from Bethany. "Sorry," the girl said. "I couldn't help myself." Tittering at Fargo, she whispered, "You gave that biddy just what she deserved."

For a ten-year-old, the girl had a remarkable sense of humor. Fargo could not help but smile. Maybe she did take after him more than he was willing to admit.

Mortimer resumed his account. "At the time, Miss Templeton was single and working as a . . . ahem . . . dancer in an establishment of ill repute. It was there that she met you, sir. Later, you took her out to eat and invited her to your hotel room." About to say more, he caught himself and cast a sideways glance at Amanda. "I trust that I need not elaborate further."

Fargo was still stumped. The details Forbush supplied could apply to more women than he cared to count. It was impossible for him to pinpoint one that matched Rosalie Templeton's description. Blue eyes. Auburn hair. Forbush might as well say she had two arms and two legs.

"Do you remember her now?" the lawyer asked hopefully.

"No."

Bethany Cole said something under her breath. Aloud, she stated, "Whether you do or you don't is irrelevant. All that is important is that you do the right thing and agree to take Mandy under your wing."

"What?" Fargo exclaimed. Were they seriously proposing that he assume the duties of being her father? After all this time? What about her mother?

Mortimer drummed his fingers. "Miss Cole, if you don't mind, allow me to finish. Mr. Fargo does not have all the facts yet. I'm afraid you'll turn him against the idea before I can present my case."

"Quit beating around the bush," Fargo said. "Why did you track me down? What is it, exactly, that you want?"

The lawyer made a tepee of his hands. "I'm sorry to have to inform you that Rosalie Templeton has gone to meet her Maker. She passed on three weeks ago. Consumption." He ruffled through the stack of papers and produced a death certificate. "Before she died, she appointed me to handle her estate, such as it is, and to safeguard Amanda until you could be found."

A sickening sensation formed in the pit of Fargo's stomach. He took several swallows, but the whiskey did not relieve it. "Rosalie Templeton wants me to take up where she left off?"

"In a nutshell, yes," Mortimer said. "I assure you that the paperwork is in order. All it takes is your signature on a few forms and Amanda can go live with you."

The girl placed her small hand on Fargo's bronzed knuckles. She adopted a yearning look and said, "Please, sir. I don't want to go to an orphanage. Some of them are terrible places, I hear. Kids my age are beaten, and worse." She tenderly squeezed. "Won't you agree to be my pa? I promise that I won't be a bother."

"But I don't even have a place where we could live," Fargo said lamely. They were all looking at him, and not one made an attempt to hide their disappointment. It didn't help that his thoughts were chaotic. A third of a bottle of whiskey on an empty stomach will do that to a man. "I need time to think this over," he said.

Huffing in resentment, the schoolmarm shifted, folded her arms, and stared off into space. "I should have known," she grated.

"Let's not treat him too harshly, shall we?" Mortimer said. "This must come as a monumental shock. And it's not as if we're asking him to take care of a dog or a cat. Being a parent is a tremendous responsibility. It's not to be taken lightly."

For once, Fargo was in complete agreement with Forbush. Mandy took her hand away and bowed her chin. Guilt washed over Fargo like surf on a beach. "No hard feelings?" he said to her. "This can't be easy on either of us."

"It isn't," the girl agreed in a small voice.

Not much was said after that. Toward the end of their meal Forbush explained how he had sent letters to lawmen and military posts west of the Mississippi, asking them to be on the lookout for the famous Trailsman. Word from a marshal in Kansas City, that Fargo had passed through there a week ago, had sent him heading west on the first stage out of St. Louis. By a sheer fluke, Fargo had stumbled on them during the holdup. "It was divine providence," Forbush said.

More like bad luck, Fargo mused. He paid for his supper, bade them good night, and collected his belongings from the desk clerk. Key in hand, he trudged up the steps.

It had been a rotten day, and the next promised to be worse. On the one hand his conscience pricked at him to do the right thing, as the schoolmarm had put it, and take custody of Mandy. But he had to be realistic. In no way, shape, or form was he ready to be a father. He could no more settle down than he could stop breathing. And he could hardly drag the girl all over creation, going wherever the wind blew them. That was no fit life for someone her age.

What was he to do?

Deep in thought, Fargo walked down the second-floor hall. Room 215 was his. He inserted the key. It grated loudly, and he entered the pitch black room. Light spilling from the corridor bathed the bed. He tossed the Henry and his saddlebags onto the quilt, then started to turn, looking for the lamp sure to be there. As he did, shadows detached themselves from the walls and pounced on him.

3

The trap was sprung a few seconds too soon. Had the three men lurking in the darkness waited until Fargo moved toward the small table in the corner to light the lantern, they would have taken him completely by surprise. As it was, Fargo's wilderness-honed reflexes were so lightning quick that he took a lithe bound backward before they laid a hand on him. That put him close to the door and squarely in the light. It also meant that to reach him, they had to spring into the open.

Fargo made a stab for his Colt, but the man on his right grabbed his arm, preventing him from drawing. He saw that none of them held a weapon, and then the other two rammed into him and he was borne to the floor with them on top.

A fist hissed at Fargo's jaw. With a wrench, he avoided the blow, and the next instant his knee connected with a groin. One of the men folded, allowing him to punch the other on the temple.

"Hold him, damn it!" snarled the attacker who had Fargo's right arm in a vise. Big and brawny, he wore a brown vest and chaps.

Swiveling, Fargo swung an uppercut. It clipped the man on the cheek as he tried to twist aside, and suddenly Fargo's right arm was free.

"Help me!" the man in the vest urged his companions.

Fargo pushed up off the floor, but he was tackled by the one he had kneed. With a resounding crash they fell against a chair. Both heaved up onto their knees. Trading blows, they battled furiously, Fargo realizing that the trio would bear him down by sheer weight of numbers if he did not get out of there right away.

As if to prove him right, the other two closed in. Fargo evaded a kick aimed at his head, gripped the culprit's ankle, and wrenched it so savagely that the man yelped. A shove sent him stumbling against another.

Momentarily in the clear, Fargo rose and backpedaled. His right hand molded to the smooth butt of his Colt, and he was sweeping the pistol out when a new element was added. A fourth gunman, a lookout, perhaps, who had been down the hall, abruptly appeared in the doorway, in a twinkling took in what had happened, and leaped on Fargo from behind.

Iron arms banded Fargo's chest, pinning his own arms to his sides. He spun, seeking to throw his assailant off, but the man clung to him like glue. As the other three converged, Fargo reversed direction, hurtling against the doorjamb.

It worked. The man on his back bore the brunt. Fargo felt the arms that held him slacken. Whipping forward, bending at the waist, he flipped the fourth man off.

Once again Fargo attempted to reach the hallway. But as he rotated, he tripped over the legs of the one he had just flipped. In vain he thrust an arm against the wall to stay upright. Down he went, to his hands and knees. A heavy form slammed into his spine. Someone seized his ankles.

Refusing to give up, Fargo rolled to the left, but was unable to tear his ankles loose. One of the hardcases grasped an arm. He was hauled to his feet, and when he cocked his other arm, that, too, was seized.

They had him. Battered and sore, Fargo struggled futilely to break their grip. The fourth man closed the door, then came around to stand in front of him.

"Don't make this any harder than it has to be, friend. Tell

us what we want to know, and you'll get out of this with all your teeth."

It was strange that all four were armed, but not one had resorted to a revolver during the fracas. Fargo had no idea what they wanted, but it was plain they were not common thieves.

The man in front of Fargo was the tallest of the bunch and as wiry as a mountain lion. He had on a black hat that crowned a thatch of equally black hair. A small scar marked his left cheek where he had been cut long ago. "Where is she?"

"Who?" Fargo responded and never glimpsed the fist that smashed into his gut. Breath whooshed from his lungs. The room spun. He would have keeled over if not for the pair who held him.

"Why make this hard on yourself, mister?" asked the tall man. "I don't enjoy beating on someone who can't fight back, but I've got my orders. My boss wants her back. And he won't let anyone or anything stand in his way."

"Let's break a few bones," suggested the bruiser holding Fargo's left arm. "That should loosen his tongue some."

The tall one shook his head. "Didn't you listen to a word the boss said? We're not to hurt this *hombre* that much if we can help it. He's not to blame. The bitch is."

A third man spoke up. "Let's just get it over with, Dixon. I hired on with this outfit to herd cattle, not to go skulkin' around hotels."

Again Dixon regarded the Trailsman. "Where is Amanda Templeton?"

Fargo had recovered enough to rejoin, "What is she to you? Why do you want her?"

"We'll ask the questions," Dixon said and slugged Fargo again. Fargo had braced himself, but even so, his stomach churned and bitter bile gushed into his mouth. "The sooner you talk, the sooner we leave."

Fargo steeled himself against the pain and spat out, "Go to hell!"

Dixon sighed. "I was hoping we could do this the easy way. I reckon I should have known better. They say you have grit." Rubbing his knuckles, he planted his legs in a wide stand, then ripped into Fargo with a series of battering punches. He knew just where to hit to cause the most pain. The punishment he inflicted was enough to reduce most men to quivering mush.

Fargo grit his teeth and rode the beating out. His ribs were on fire, and his gut was a seething cauldron of intense suffering when his tormenter finished. But his will to resist was as strong as ever.

Dixon panted from his exertion. "Had enough?" he asked. "Ready to talk?"

"Don't make me laugh. I've met women who hit harder than you do," Fargo said. It resulted in another round of punishing blows that left him so weak he could hardly stand. But he was still defiant. Wheezing, he sagged and declared, "The next time we meet, you had better be heeled."

The man in the brown vest swore. "This is getting us nowhere. Let's sneak him out the back and go off into the woods. We'll tie him to a tree and take turns with a whip. I guarantee that will make him talk."

Unexpectedly, a knock sounded on the door. The four men stiffened, and Dixon dropped a hand to his Remington.

"Mr. Fargo? Are you in there?"

It was Bethany Cole. Fargo straightened and was going to shout a warning, but a hand was pressed over his mouth. He bit down with all his might, his front teeth shearing sinew and grinding into bone. The gunman yelped.

Evidently the schoolmarm misconstrued what she heard and opened the door, saying, "What was that? I didn't quite catch—" She saw the four men. One lunged at her, but she skipped out of reach and hollered, "Help! Help! A man is being robbed!"

At the outcry Dixon cursed lustily and darted from the room, shouting, "Come on, before she brings the law down on our heads!" Boots pounding, the quartet fled, the last man looking at Fargo as he dashed out and warning, "You haven't seen the last of us. We'll be watching."

Shouts had broken out up and down the corridor. Fargo took a few faltering steps after the four, but his legs were not up to it. Staggering to the edge of the bed, he sat down before he fell. A dress rustled close by and light blazed.

Bethany had lit the lamp. "How badly are you hurt?" she asked, coming over.

A commotion erupted right outside the room. Heads were framed in the doorway.

"What was all the yelling about?" someone inquired.

"Who were those men?" asked another.

The schoolmarm took it on herself to say, "They broke into this man's room, probably seeking valuables to steal. It's fortunate that I came along when I did or there is no telling what they would have done."

"Mister, are you okay?" a natty gent said. "Want one of us to fetch the marshal?"

Fargo quelled the pangs lancing his abdomen long enough to reply, "No, that won't be necessary. They were scared off before they could steal anything." Involving the law was not to his liking. The marshal was bound to pester him with questions to which he had no answers and might try to stop him from tracking the four down on his own.

Gradually, the other guests dispersed. Bethany poured water from a white pitcher into a basin, dampened a washcloth, and applied it to his forehead.

Fargo saw no need to mention that it was his midsection that hurt the most. "Thanks," he said and arched a brow. "Don't take this wrong, but what the hell are you doing here? I thought you hated me?"

Bethany was crossing to the upended chair. Pausing, she gave him an odd sort of smile. "Hate is a strong word. I can't say I've ever hated anyone. But I have intensely disliked a few people now and then."

"There's a difference?"

She set the chair upright and sank onto it, unconscious of the supple alluring flow of her body, the enticing swell of her thighs. She had a sensual vitality about her that no prim exterior could fully conceal. "I didn't come here to discuss my feelings toward you. I came to talk about Amanda."

Groaning, Fargo lay back. Maybe if he pretended to be gravely hurt, she would go away and badger him some other time. "I haven't made up my mind yet. You'll get my answer tomorrow."

"Be so kind as to not insult my intelligence, and I won't insult yours," the schoolmarm said. "We both know that you have no intention of becoming that girl's rightful guardian. She will end up in an overcrowded orphanage in St. Louis, her whole life ruined. All because you are too selfish to put her welfare before your own."

"Here we go again," Fargo muttered. Closing his eyes, he said, "Do me a favor and go make someone else's life miserable. I've had a long day, and I'd like to get some rest."

"I'm afraid you can't get rid of me that easily. I'm not leaving until you give me your word that you will honor Rosalie Templeton's memory by rearing your child."

"*Her* child," Fargo set the schoolmarm straight. "I doubt that I ever met Rosalie."

"It's been ten years. Can you look me in the eyes and say with absolute certainty that you never did?" Bethany countered. His refusal to do so sparked an unladylike snort of satisfaction. "I didn't think so."

Covering his eyes with a forearm, Fargo let her prattle on about the need for a young girl to have a decent home. How children raised without parents had a much harder time of it than those who came from loving families. He paid no attention until she made a remark about herself.

"I know what I'm talking about, Mr. Fargo. My mother and father were killed in a wagon accident when I was only five. Since none of our relatives wanted me, I was dumped in an orphanage. The next ten years were the worst of my life. The man who ran it skimped on food, on clothes, on everything. His staff beat those who acted up and threw us into closets for days at a time as extra punishment. It was hell on earth."

Fargo looked at her in a whole new light. Now he understood why she was meddling, why Mandy's future was so important to her. "Has Forbush mentioned that someone else is interested in the girl?"

"No. Who?"

"That's what I would like to learn." Rising, Fargo moved to the open door and motioned. "Out you go, Miss Cole. Look me up first thing in the morning, and you can bend my ear all you want."

The schoolmarm was flabbergasted. "You're throwing me out?"

"More or less." Fargo admired how her bosom swelled as her anger mounted. She thrust to her feet and stormed toward him, and he half figured she would slap him as she went by. But all she did was glare. The musky, tantalizing scent of her perfume lingered long after she had tromped off.

Closing the door, Fargo blew out the lamp and glided to the window. Crouching to one side, he peeked between the edge of the curtain and the window frame. It was early yet, and traffic on the street was heavy. Carriages, riders, pedestrians, all flowed in a steady stream. Across from the Excelsior was a mercantile. An alley flanked it on both sides. And in the mouth of the alley on the left lounged two men who were more interested in the hotel than in the passersby. One of them happened to light a cigarette. In the flare of the match a brown vest and chaps were visible.

Fargo headed for the hall. So the quartet had meant what they said about watching him! He checked both ways before slipping out and locking the door. Turning left instead of right, he soon came to a narrow flight of steps. At the bottom was the hotel's rear door. Rarely used, it opened onto Fremont Street. Again he checked in both directions before blending into the flow of people who were bearing to the east.

He traveled two blocks before turning right, covered another two blocks, and turned right again. Presently, he drew near the alley bordering the mercantile, but at the opposite end from the two watchers. Going past it, he saw that it was crammed with discarded crates and boxes and assorted trash.

Wheeling, Fargo ducked into the alley's mouth, his back to a wall. The hubbub in the street smothered any slight sounds he made as he stalked toward the unsuspecting pair. Keeping low, often in a crouch, he was soon within earshot, hidden behind a stack of empty produce crates.

The man in the vest was idly puffing on his cigarette while his smaller friend chipped at the wall of the mercantile with a pocket knife.

"This bores me to death, Jessie," the smaller man said with a Texas twang. "Why did Darnell have to pick us to help out? I can think of twenty things I'd rather be doin' than standin' here twiddlin' my thumbs."

"Quit your griping, Carver," the man in the vest said. "What the boss wants, he gets. If you don't like it, you can always quit and go back to San Antonio."

"No thanks. I've had my fill of herdin' cattle for a livin'. Workin' for Darnell ain't half as hard." Carver gouged his knife into the wood. "What do you make of this whole business, anyhow? That woman done him wrong, I suppose, but—"

"You *suppose*?" Jessie said with starch in his tone. "Don't be judging others until you've walked a mile in their boots. Darnell did what he had to. We do what we have to. It's as simple as that."

"Why are you gettin' so crotchety on me? You heard their spats the same as me. Hell, he's about busted every piece of furniture in the mansion at one time or another. The man has a worse temper than a longhorn."

Jessie exhaled a ring of smoke. "Don't let him hear you

say that, pard. He doesn't like those who work for him to flap their gums about him behind his back."

"Excuse me all to hell," Carver groused.

Fargo was only ten feet away. His aim was to march them into the alley at gunpoint and persuade them to reveal everything they knew. The arrival of a third party spoiled his plan.

The newcomer was dressed in the height of fashion, including a tall-crowned silk top hat popular back East. Flourishing a cane that had a snake-head handle crafted from solid ivory, he said without ceremony, "Mr. Darnell requires your presence at the house he has rented, gentlemen. Do you know how to get there?"

"Sure do, greenhorn," Carver said. "You're the one who gets lost all the time, as I recollect."

"I admit to being inexperienced in the wilderness," the man in the top hat said, "but I know my way around this city far better than you do, Texan." Twirling his cane, he ambled off. "I must inform the others. Please be prompt. Mr. Darnell does not tolerate tardiness."

Carver folded his knife and stuck it into a pants pocket. "That *hombre* rubs me the wrong way. One of these days I'm goin' to teach him some respect."

Jessie stretched and remarked, "You do, and you'll regret it. Trevane has been Darnell's right-hand man for years."

"Does that give him the right to look down his nose at us?" Carver asked, then answered his own question. "No, it doesn't. Yet he treats us as if we're hicks from the backwoods."

"What else did you expect? Trevane was born and bred in New York City, I hear."

"That explains it. Those New Yorkers are always puttin' on airs," Carver said. "Must be all that sooty air in the winter. It clogs their brains so they can't think straight."

The pair hiked westward. Fargo silently counted to ten, then advanced to the corner of the mercantile. They were crossing to the other side of the street, Carver keeping a hawkish eye on his hotel window.

Fargo stayed on the south side and trailed them. By hanging half a block back and always looking away when one or the other glanced over a shoulder, he was not spotted. They turned only twice, the last instance taking them into a residential area notable for huge homes and verdant gardens. It was where Jefferson City's well-to-do lived.

Far fewer souls were abroad. Fargo had to exercise more care not to be caught. He let their lead increase to a block, but still kept them in sight. They were more relaxed now that the city was behind them. Neither hardly ever looked back.

It was not long before Fargo saw that they were making for a low promontory. The immense dwelling on it commanded a panoramic view of the entire city. Light shone in every window. Marble columns fronted walls covered with ivy. A closed wrought-iron gate was guarded by two men in suits, both armed with shotguns and revolvers.

In the shadow of a willow Fargo stopped. The guards opened the gate for Carver and Jessie, who strolled up a winding gravel lane to the house. Whoever this Darnell was, Fargo reflected, he had money—lots and lots of it.

Carver pumped a brass knocker, and the door was opened by a servant.

Fargo needed to get onto the grounds. But in addition to the guards, they protected by a ten-foot-high wall. Retracing his steps until he could circle wide without being seen, he approached the estate from the north. Here there were fewer neighbors, fewer people, and no gate. At the base of the wall he craned his neck, coiled, and leaped with outflung arms. It did no good. The wall was too high.

Fargo prowled to the east. In the distance a dog barked, leading him to wonder if there were any on the grounds of the estate. He had tangled with watchdogs before and had no hankering to do so again.

More ivy covered the northeast corner. Fargo tested it

and decided it would bear his weight. But at that instant a carriage clattered around an intersection a hundred yards away and came toward him. Flattening, he removed his hat and buried his face in the grass, leaving one eye exposed.

The driver was admiring the stars. He flicked his whip as he passed the corner. Inside, a man and a woman cuddled.

Fargo did not rise until they were well gone. Jamming his hat back on, he gripped the ivy, hooked a boot into the thick mass, and climbed. At any moment he thought it might give way under his weight, but he reached the top without incident. Spreading out on the rim, he surveyed the grounds. A rose garden flourished near the house. Closer to him stood a white gazebo. Empty, it seemed.

The silhouette of a man appeared in a third-floor window. Fargo had the impression that the man was gazing out over the lawn. He was thankful there was no moon and that scattered low clouds added to the gloom.

When the silhouette moved off, Fargo dropped, bending his knees so he landed lightly. He angled toward the gazebo, relying on shrubbery to conceal him. Suddenly, he halted. The odor of cigar or pipe smoke hung heavy in the air, tingling his nose.

In the gazebo someone coughed.

Fargo hunkered, his hand on the Colt. A few gray wisps marked the position of the smoker. Fargo debated whether to swing to the left and go around, or whether he should rap the man on the skull. The decision was made for him by the opening of a mansion door. Three men emerged and filed down a narrow path.

The smoker stood and stepped into the starlight. A large, broad-shouldered man, he puffed on his pipe as they hurried toward him, shrouding his features in smoke. "Well?" he demanded in the manner of a man accustomed to having others do his bidding. "Where is she?"

Two of the three were men Fargo had seen earlier. One was Trevane, the dandy with the cane. The other was

Jessie. The third was a scarecrow with a sallow complexion whose clothes hung loosely on his thin frame.

Jessie responded. "We tried, Mr. Darnell, but we couldn't make him talk. Then a woman showed up, and we had to make ourselves scarce or we would have had the law down on our heads."

"I do not tolerate failure, Mr. Hinson."

Fargo crept to the right to see better. He wanted a good look at Darnell. At a gap in the shrubbery, he halted and felt his blood chill when the hammer of a gun clicked close to his ear and a gravel voice boomed loud and clear.

"Don't you so much as twitch, stranger, or you're a dead man."

4

The element of surprise can work both ways. Naturally, the man who had caught Skye Fargo off guard figured that Fargo would do what anyone with common sense would do, and stand rock still. But he had no way of knowing that he was dealing with someone whose pantherish speed and courage were talked about in saloons and taverns all across the growing country. Talked about, and envied.

Fargo knew that the gunman was behind him, and he had a fair idea where the pistol was, even though he could not see it. Based on the sound of the click, he guessed that the revolver was close to the left side of his head and slightly behind his left ear.

All this Fargo realized in the blink of an eye. Like a mountain lion brought to bay, he whirled away from the pistol and swung his arm up and out. It connected with a wrist. The six-gun went off, the slug tearing harmlessly into the soil at his feet. Fargo saw a bearded face, eyes wide in disbelief. His fist, crashing into the man's jaw, took him out of the frying pan and into the fire.

For Darnell and the three underlings had spun at the guard's outcry. Now Darnell bellowed, "Someone is on the grounds! Get him!", and Trevane, Jessie and the scarecrow bounded toward the shrubbery, Jessie and the scarecrow unlimbering hardware.

From the house rose shouts. Figures appeared in the rear doorway.

Cursing, Fargo pivoted and ran. Gunfire crackled. Lead

whizzed past. Glancing back, he saw fireflies flare in front of the scarecrow so he answered in kind and the scarecrow toppled. Jessie fanned off two shots that nipped at Fargo's hat.

Trevane had disappeared, but Darnell had not moved. Boldly, imperiously, he stood in the open, apparently confident that no one would dare shoot him. Either the man was recklessly brave, or the biggest fool in all creation.

Men were pouring from the house. Several carried rifles.

Fargo plunged through the shrubbery, trampling plants and flowers. Limbs and thorns plucked at his buckskins. He dashed around a shoulder-high bush just as a rifle blasted. The shot came much too close for Fargo's liking. Darnell's men were good. But then, anyone as wealthy as Darnell could afford to hire the best.

Jessie was gaining. To discourage him, Fargo turned and fired and saw Jessie dive flat. Racing on, Fargo flew past the last of the shrubs. Before him was the corner of the wall and the thick ivy. Holstering the Colt, he paused to reach for a handhold.

Fargo could not say what it was that warned him. Perhaps a whisper of sound. Perhaps a hint of motion. Perhaps intuition. Whatever the case, he wheeled and dropped into a crouch.

It was well he did. Had Fargo been standing fully upright, he would have lost his head to the vicious swing of Trevane's sword. It whistled above him, the blade glinting dully in the dim light.

The dandy's cane was actually a sword cane, the ivory snake-head actually the handle at the end of two and a half feet of razor sharp steel. As calmly as if he were engaged in a formal fencing match, Trevane gracefully sidestepped and flicked the tapered point straight out.

Fargo was backing up. He bumped into the wall, and with nowhere to go, dodged to the right. The point ripped into his shoulder, shearing the buckskin but not his skin. Trevane smoothly snapped the sword back to try again.

The pounding of heavy feet in the shrubbery and the shouts of those closing in galvanized Fargo into taking a short, swift step, and planting the instep of his right boot where it would hurt Trevane the most.

The dandy yipped and covered his groin, then tottered to one side, wheezing, "That was a foul blow, sir! You are no gentleman!"

Fargo had no time to point out that when a man was fighting for his life, proper rules of conduct went out the window. Turning, he vaulted as high as he could and snagged trailing vines. Scrambling upward, he heard the panting of a man who was almost to the wall. Jessie, probably. His right hand closed on the top and he heaved himself upward. At the same split second, a pistol banged, the slug whining off the wall near his elbow.

With a monumental heave, Fargo hauled himself up and over. The six-shooter spoke again, but he was shielded by the rim and the bullet only gouged a furrow next to his hand. He fell, twisting in midair to alight on his feet. Landing, he sped eastward.

Down the street was a wooded area, a park, maybe, or undeveloped land. He suspected that Darnell would not be content with chasing him off the estate. Yells from the top of the wall and the *thud* of bodies dropping to the grass outside it confirmed his hunch.

Fargo pumped his legs, furious at the quirk of fate that had spoiled his plan. Everything had gone to hell. Instead of learning why Darnell was so interested in Amanda Templeton, he would be lucky if he got out of there with his hide intact. He angled onto the road so he could run faster, but it proved to be a mistake.

"There he goes!"

"Bring him down!"

Pistols blistered the night with a thunderous din. All around Fargo, lead buzzed and hummed. He weaved to make himself harder to hit.

"After him! He's getting away!"

That last sounded like Trevane. A glance showed Fargo five or six men were in pursuit, with more dropping from the wall. Darnell must have a small army at his command. Eluding them would not be easy. Pumping his legs, he came to the wooded tract and lost himself amid the trees.

For the moment Fargo was safe. He concentrated on putting distance between the gunmen and himself. Scant undergrowth was to be found, which enabled him to move rapidly although it would work against him if he had to seek cover.

The trees were mainly maples and oaks, with occasional willows thrown in. Their long branches formed a verdant canopy above him, blotting out even the dim starlight. He ran in a twilight realm of gloom and inky shadow.

There was a chance that the gunshots would bring the marshal or a town constable to investigate. But it was a slim one. The estate was so far from the middle of town that it was doubtful they aroused much interest. Nor could Fargo count on any of Darnell's few neighbors going to all the trouble of saddling up and riding in to report the racket. In Missouri, folks tended to mind their own affairs more religiously than elsewhere.

No, Fargo was on his own. Pausing to take his bearings, he replaced the cartridges he had used. From the street came the slap of leather soles and furtive movement. He sprinted deeper into the woods, gliding from tree trunk to tree trunk, relying on the skills taught him by his Indian friends to move as noiselessly as a ghost. That was his edge. Few men could match his wilderness savvy.

Another minute went by. Then two. Fargo began to think that he had given his pursuers the slip and would soon be free to head for the hotel, when ahead of him a twig broke with a distinct *crack.*

An animal? Or more of Darnell's men? Fargo couldn't see how any of them could have gotten ahead of him, unless another bunch had come from the front of the estate. If so, he was trapped between the two groups. Halting beside a broad willow, he scoured the murky woodland, his keen eyes detecting furtive figures spread out in a long line less than twenty yards away. They were warily advancing. Several would pass close by the willow.

Now Fargo knew how a fox felt when it was hemmed in by hounds. He could break to the right or left, but they were bound to spot him. He'd be caught in a deadly crossfire. Desperate, he glanced around, then bent his head back. A glimmer of hope took root.

Sliding the Colt into his holster, Fargo rose onto the tips of his toes and extended his arms. His fingers fell just shy of the lowest limb. Hopping, he caught hold, braced his boots against the trunk, and pulled himself into the willow. Clambering higher, he shifted to the left side of the tree and crawled out onto a thick limb partially hidden by others. He stretched out flat, clamping his ankles on either side of it and looping his left arm for added measure.

It seemed insane to just lie there while a dozen or more gunmen stalked through the woods, seeking his life. But there was a crafty method to Fargo's seeming insanity. For as any hunter knew, most animals rarely paid much attention to what was above them. They took it for granted that trees were the domain of birds and insects and other harmless wildlife. It was why many hunters, deer hunters in particular, liked to perch in a high roost and wait for their quarry to wander by.

The same was true of human beings, to a degree. Few ever bothered to look up. The trees above them were their blind side, so to speak.

Fargo, clinging to the stout limb, spotted two gunmen slowly making their way toward him. Both constantly scanned to the right and the left. Neither thought to crane his neck upward.

The other figures were blurred outlines in the gloom. They made little noise, though far more than Indians would. The lone exception was a grizzled frontiersman in worn buckskins, armed with a Sharps. He was off to the east a ways, and he never so much as rustled a blade of grass or stirred a leaf. He was also the only one who did bother to look up now and again, but he was not near enough to the willow to pose a threat. Or so Fargo hoped.

A lanky gunman approached the tree. His revolver swung from side to side. An arm's length from the trunk, and directly under Fargo, he halted to push back his hat and mop his brow.

Fargo mimicked marble. He watched the gunman out of the corner of his eye rather than risk staring right at the man. The Sioux had taught him that some people could sense when they were being stared at, and experience had proven them right. Some men and women had an uncanny knack for knowing when they were being spied on.

The lanky gunman started to go on, then paused. Acting uncertain, he rotated to study the woods behind him, then the woods in front. He scratched his temple, shrugged, and took another step. Something brought him up short again, however, and he started to turn.

Fargo had a gut feeling that the gunman had sensed his presence. He just knew that the man was going to glance up and see him, and he braced to push off and drop. Suddenly, the woods to the north were shattered by a shout, "There he is!" Guns roared, to be answered by the men who had come from the south. Over the bedlam a man bellowed angrily, but no one could hear what he said.

The lanky gunman darted behind the willow and entered the fray, firing at elusive targets. Neither he nor any of his companions realized the mistake they had made.

Slugs were flying thick and furious. Fargo prayed that none of the stray lead found him. The gunmen were doing more damage to the trees than they were to their imagined enemies. He heard a bullet smack into the hole near his feet. Another ripped a leaf from a branch at his shoulder.

At the height of the firing, the lanky gunman leaned to the right and took precise aim. An invisible blow punched him halfway around, and he grunted like a stricken bull.

50

Staggering, he touched a palm to the front of his shirt. When he lowered it, a dark stain covered his hand. "No!" he said and tottered against the trunk. His knees buckled. Like molten wax oozing down the side of a candle, he oozed to the ground and sat gaping dully at his palm.

The initial flurry of wild shots died down. In the temporary lull, as the gunmen reloaded, an irate voice screeched, "Stop firing, you jackasses! You're shooting at one another!" He paused. "Weasel, is that you over there?"

"Yep," answered the grizzled frontiersman. "Trevane, is that you?"

"Who else, you hayseed!"

No more shots boomed out. In the awkward silence that followed, acrid gunsmoke drifted through the trees. Some swirled around the lanky gunman. He coughed, spitting blood. Slumping, he sagged, his face rising to trace the flight of the smoke. In so doing, he spotted Fargo.

The Trailsman swooped a hand to his pistol. All it would take was a single outcry and he was as good as dead. There must be twenty killers nearby. Too many for him to fight his way through.

The gunman opened his mouth. He sat up, his eyelids fluttering as he struggled to voice the shout he yearned to voice. Before he died, he wanted more than anything to let his friends know where Fargo was. His eyes, his posture, his frantic fight to live a few more moments, were proof of that. From his throat gurgled a word that was strangled into a groan, choked by a rising scarlet flood that gushed over his quivering lower lip. His shout became a whimper. His arm shaking, he tried to raise his revolver. It proved too heavy. His arm flopped as life left him, and he buckled, his head tilting until his forehead rested on the ground.

"Over here! Banner has been hit!"

A blond gunman rushed to the dead man's side. Rolling him onto his back, the blond man felt for a pulse as others swarmed over. In moments they were standing four deep around Banner, Trevane, Jessie, and Weasel in front.

"He's dead," the blond gunman told the dandy.

Trevane gestured in contempt. "It serves him right." He glowered at the cutthroats. "It serves all of you right. This is what happens when you don't use your heads. How many times has Mr. Darnell told you to think, think, think!" Trevane shoved through the ring, smoothed a ruffled sleeve, and said, "Honestly, gentlemen. All of us against one man, and he manages to slip right through our fingers. Mr. Darnell will be most displeased." Tossing his head, he walked off.

The dour looks cast at the dandy's retreating rigid back revealed to Fargo that Trevane was despised by Darnell's other men. A comment by Weasel explained why.

"That damned citified upstart! Thinks he's so much better than the rest of us! If it weren't for Darnell, I'd whittle him down a peg or two."

"You'd have to wait in line, old-timer," declared a surly character in the garb of a riverman, who tapped a long knife strapped to his hip. "I'd like to stake him out and skin him alive."

"I never did understand what the boss sees in him," said another. "Darnell should send Trevane back to New York, where he belongs."

The knot broke up. Men drifted singly and in small clusters toward the estate.

"Hold up, you yacks!" Weasel said. "Some of us have to tote Banner on back. We don't want any of the locals to stumble on the body. Darnell would have a fit if the law was to get involved."

The frontiersman pointed to three men, who helped him lift the body and carry it off. A fourth man picked up Banner's hat, which had slipped off, and began to follow. He went a few feet past the branch Fargo was on, then inexplicably stopped.

Fargo feared a repeat of what had happened with Banner. He loosened the Colt, but the man produced the makings and proceeded to roll a cigarette. The rest were almost out of sight before the gunman finished, struck a match against his boot, and took deep drags to kindle his smoke. Sighing in contentment, the killer ambled off, humming to himself.

Five minutes passed before Fargo stirred. Grasping the limb with both hands, he swung off, dangled, and dropped. He had much to think over as he made a beeline to the east. Since he would not put it past Darnell to have men search for him, he took a roundabout route back to the Excelsior, arriving at the rear of the hotel well past midnight.

The halls were as quiet as the inside of a tomb. Fargo crept to the second floor and along the hall to his room. It was impossible to open the door without making noise, so he didn't try. Unlocking it quickly, he pushed the door wide, his pistol out and cocked.

Someone was there, seated primly on the bed, hands in her lap, looking as fresh and perky as a daisy. But it was the last person Fargo expected.

It was Amanda Templeton.

Bewildered, Fargo double-checked the room. No one else was there. "What the—?" he said, and caught himself before he swore.

"Hello, Pa," the girl said. "Where have you been? I've been waiting an awful long time, and I was getting worried something had happened to you."

"Do you know what time it is?" Fargo demanded, closing the door halfway. "You have no business being here in the middle of the night."

Mandy shrugged. "We need to talk, Pa. I waited until Miss Cole was asleep and snuck on out. Please don't tell her what I've done or she'll give me another lecture."

Fargo had half a mind to shoo her back to the room she shared with the schoolmarm anyway, but curiosity got the better of him. "About what, little one?"

"About us." Mandy rested her elbows on her knees and her chin in her hands. "I want you to know that I can't wait for us to go off together."

She said it so happily that Fargo felt guilty saying, "Don't go putting the cart before the horse. We don't know for sure yet that I am your father."

"You're praying it isn't you, aren't you?"

What was a man to do? Fargo asked himself. The last thing he wanted was to hurt the child's feeling. But at the same time, it wouldn't be wise to build up her hopes and have them dashed later on. "If it turns out that I'm your pa, we'll take it from there," he said. "As yet, there is no proof that I am. All I have is your mother's word. And I'll be honest with you. I don't remember her at all."

"It's been a long time," Mandy said, adding impishly, "Everyone has heard about you and your fancy way with the ladies. I'll bet the famous Trailsman can't recall all the women he's known."

It gave Fargo pause. For someone so young, her comment was downright strange. It was almost as if she were quoting words someone else had uttered. "Where did you hear that? From your mother?"

For some reason Mandy averted her gaze and said a little too quickly, "No. Ma didn't talk much about you until the very end. When I was small, she never would tell me who my pa was. It was a big secret."

"Were the two of you close?"

The girl acted offended by the question. "Of course. I'd do anything for Ma. She was always there when I needed her. She never let me down."

"You must miss her a lot," Fargo remarked. She nodded once. That was all. No sorrow twisted her features. No tears flowed. There was no reaction whatsoever, which was so peculiar that the germ of doubt festering deep within Fargo doubled in size. "You do, don't you?"

"My ma was the best," Mandy said and brightened. "One day I'll see her again. She promised me, before she went away. She said that nothing will keep us apart."

The pledge was the kind of thing a church-going woman might say, so Fargo absently asked, "What church did your mother go to?" Any tidbit he could learn about the woman, however trivial, might be the clue he needed to jar his memory. To his surprise, the girl laughed.

"Ma never went to church. Ever. She said it was for folks who liked to look down their noses at others. She wouldn't be caught dead in one."

Something did not add up. Fargo began to pace, mulling what he had learned. "Tell me more about her," he urged. "What was she like? What were her interests?"

Normally, children loved to talk about a parent. But Mandy was different. Shaking her head, she said, "I didn't come here to talk about Ma. I want to talk about us. What can I do to prove to you that I'm your daughter?"

"Nothing," Fargo said frankly.

Mandy slid off the bed and came over to hug him. "If you say so. But, Pa, I'm so glad that we found you! It will be wonderful to do things together, won't it? You can take me riding and to the theater and all sorts of fun places. We'll never be apart again."

Fargo patted her head, at a loss for words. "Let's get you back to your own room," he said. Impulsively, she clasped his hand and steered him out the door. Since the schoolmarm was staying just down the hall, he did not bother locking his door. When they got to her room, he lifted the latch quietly and gave the girl another pat as she slipped on by.

Pausing, Mandy blew him a kiss. "We have a lot of making up to do, Pa," she whispered. The rosy glow of the hall lamp, bathing her upturned face, lent her the innocence of an angel.

An odd lump formed in Fargo's throat. "Be sure and lock the door," he said more gruffly than he intended. Once she did, he returned to his own room and not only locked the door but propped the chair against it, then plopped onto the bed. It had been a long, grueling day.

Was he truly the girl's father? That thought swirled around and around in his brain until a fitful sleep claimed him, a sleep haunted by a recurring nightmare in which a thousand women dressed in black, each holding a bundled infant, pointed accusing fingers at him and cried with one voice, "You're the one! You! You! You!"

5

Skye Fargo was washing his face and chest early the next morning when a knock sounded on his door. Taking the white towel from its peg, he began to dry himself as he crossed the room. "Who is it?"

"It's me, Pa," Mandy called out. "And Miss Cole."

Fargo opened the door. Amanda wore a crisp yellow dress and hat and showed him more teeth than a patent medicine man trying to make a hard sell. The schoolmarm wore a brown dress that clung to the lush contours of her superbly molded body. Her eyes roved to his hard, muscular chest, and down over his knotted abdomen. He saw her throat bob and suppressed a grin. "Morning, ladies."

"Get ready, Pa," Mandy said, filing inside without being asked. "We're taking you to breakfast. Mr. Forbush will join us in the dining room."

"That is, if you want to come," Bethany Cole added.

Smiling, Fargo finished drying, saying, "Only an idiot would refuse an invitation from two such lovely ladies." His eyes lingered on Bethany as he said it, and her cheeks grew pink. Slipping on his shirt, he combed his hair, donned his hat, strapped on the Colt, and was ready to go.

Mandy assumed the lead. With trim, measured steps, her proud head held high, one small hand holding Fargo's, she escorted him to the dining room. She had a confident, adult poise about her that Fargo could not help but marvel at.

Mortimer J. Forbush, attorney-at-law, awaited them at the same corner table they had sat at the night before. He wore the same suit and the same bowler. Doffing it to the schoolmarm, he went to hold a chair out for her, but Fargo stepped in and did the honors.

Bethany Cole gave him a look that plainly revealed it was the last thing in the world she ever imagined he would do. "Thank you," she said demurely. "It's nice to know that somewhere in that barbarian body of yours is the heart of a true gentleman."

Fargo could not resist. "I didn't think you had noticed my body much," he said. His thrust hit home. She blushed darker than she had upstairs and hastily took her seat.

Forbush impatiently tapped the table while the waitress took their order, and the moment she turned away, he lifted his valise off the floor and opened it in his lap. "Now then," he said eagerly. "I have the papers all set for you to sign, Mr. Fargo. I even took the liberty of bringing a pen and ink."

"You're taking it for granted what my answer will be," Fargo noted.

The lawyer glanced up sharply. "Well, I naturally figured that you would not want this poor child to languish in an orphanage for God knows how long." He licked his lips. "Do you mean to say, then, that you do not accept guardianship?"

Fargo saw that the girl and the schoolmarm were hanging on every word. "I haven't made up my mind yet."

"But last evening you assured us that you would let us know today," Forbush protested.

"I've changed my mind," Fargo said and let them stew a bit before he elaborated. "Mandy and her mother spent quite a few years in St. Louis, I take it?"

Forbush's eyes narrowed. "Mandy was born and raised there, yes. Rosalie moved to St. Louis from Ohio when she was six or seven. Why?"

"Then there must be a lot of people in St. Louis who knew Rosalie fairly well," Fargo said. He observed how the lawyer's one hand squeezed the valise handle so tight, the knuckles turned white.

"I would guess so," Mortimer hedged. "But I fail to see the significance."

"It's simple," Fargo said. "Being a parent isn't something to be taken lightly. I'd like to learn more about Rosalie before I make up my mind."

"What do you intend to do?" Mortimer asked, but it was apparent that he had already guessed and just as apparent that he was not pleased.

"I'm going to St. Louis to talk to people who knew Mandy's mother," Fargo said. "Mandy will go along and introduce them to me."

The lawyer and the girl exchanged looks. Mortimer coughed a few times, then said, "I'm afraid I can't permit that. The poor child has been through so much recently. Dragging her back to the city where her mother passed on will dredge up too many bitter memories. I can't put her through such misery again."

Fargo leaned forward and lowered his voice to a steely growl. "You make it sound as if you have a choice."

Forbush drew back, his mouth falling open. "Now see here," he blustered. "I take that as some sort of threat."

Slowly, for effect, Fargo slid the Colt out and set it on the table with a *thump*. Resting his hand on the butt, he locked eyes with the law wrangler. "Take it any way you want."

For a few moments tension thick enough to be cut with a knife hung heavy in the air. The lawyer glared. Mandy squirmed. Bethany Cole, to everyone's amazement, came to Fargo's defense.

"I don't think Mr. Fargo is being unreasonable," she told Forbush. "Wouldn't you want to learn all you could about Rosalie if you were in his place?" Bethany smiled at Mandy. "What do you say, dear? Wouldn't it be best for your father to learn all he can about your mother?"

Amanda glanced at Forbush, then down at her lap. "I

suppose," she said softly. "But I don't cotton to going back there. It will make me cry a lot."

"Don't fret yourself," Bethany said. "I'll be along to comfort you."

Fargo and Forbush both turned and said at the same time, "What?"

"You heard me," Bethany declared. "I'm not letting this poor girl out of my sight until this is settled one way or the other. Luckily, I have plenty of free time on my hands. I can be her chaperone for as long as need be."

"How wonderful," Mortimer said, but he did not sound as if he truly believed it was.

"There's no need, ma'am," Mandy said. "Mr. Forbush will look after me. Not that I need him to. I'm a big girl. I can handle myself."

Bethany patted the child's arm. "I'm sure you can, dear. But it's not fitting for someone of your tender years to be in the company of a notorious reprobate without someone to look after you."

Fargo bristled. Half a minute ago he had wanted to hug her for speaking up in his behalf. Now he wanted to slug her. "Just what the hell does that mean?" he demanded.

Unruffled, the schoolmarm bestowed a smirk. "Your reputation speaks for itself."

"Now hold on—" Fargo began, indignant.

Bethany Cole lifted a hand to silence him. "Please don't be offended. I know that you would never do anything to harm this precious girl. But others might not be so understanding. I have your best interests at heart. Trust me."

Ironically, she was the only one there Fargo did trust. "I have no objections," he begrudged her.

"And you, Mr. Forbush?" Bethany asked.

"Whatever you want," the lawyer sulked. "I don't seem to have much say in any of this."

Fargo had been waiting for the right moment to pose a question. With Forbush's guard down, the time was ripe.

"Before I forget, what do you know about a man called Darnell?"

Mortimer was tilting a glass to his mouth. For no apparent reason it slipped, and he spilled some water down the front of his shirt and jacket. Righting the glass, he picked up his napkin and wiped his clothes. "Goodness gracious," he said. "I must be half asleep yet." He did not answer until he was done. "Darnell, you say? Offhand, I can't think of anyone with that name. Who is he?"

Fargo had seen Amanda's eyes widen at the mention of the man who was so interested in her. She had promptly pretended to be fascinated by a painting on the wall. But he wasn't fooled. "I was hoping *you* could tell me," he said.

Bethany was the only one who had not behaved oddly. She was also the only one to say, "I seem to recall hearing that name before. But I can't remember where."

"If it comes to you, let me know," Fargo said. The waitress was heading for their table, carrying their food. He rubbed his palms in anticipation. Breakfast was his favorite meal. A half-dozen eggs, half a pound of bacon, and a pot of coffee would start his day off right. "Eat up," he said. "After we're done, we're all taking a short ride."

"To where?" Forbush inquired.

"You'll see," was all the further Fargo would commit himself.

Their conversation dried up. Fargo was too busy cramming food into his mouth to hold up his end. He was a robust, virile man, and he had appetites to match. The others had long been done when he pushed back his plate after his third helping and patted his stomach. "I'll have to remember to stop here again the next time I pass through Jefferson City."

Mortimer J. Forbush had picked at his food and barely taken three sips of his coffee. He was the last to rise and straggled after the rest to the lobby. Only once did he speak, and that was when he bent to whisper in Mandy's ear. The girl listened intently, and nodded.

A line of carriages awaited the pleasure of the Hotel Excelsior's patrons. There were broughams, landaulettes, victorias, and more. Fargo selected a six-passenger phaeton with a canopy, and helped the women on.

"Where to, sir?" the coachman inquired, hefting his slender whip.

"I'll guide you as we go," Fargo said, which had to suffice because he did not know the names of half the streets he had traveled the night previous. And in the light of day, everything was different. He only hoped his sense of direction would not let him down.

Certain landmarks, trees, buildings, walls, and the like helped immensely. Twice they took wrong turns and Fargo had the driver backtrack. None of the others made a comment, but he could see they were puzzled.

Traffic was heavy, even in the residential area. The phaeton went through an intersection, and when Fargo happened to gaze to his right, he spied the mansion on the low promontory. "There!" he pointed. "That's where we're going."

If Fargo was counting on some sort of reaction from the lawyer or Mandy, he was sorely disappointed. Neither showed any nervousness as the carriage clattered toward the wrought iron gate flanked by stone pillars.

Fargo was taking a calculated gamble. By having Forbush and Amanda confront Darnell, he hoped to get to the bottom of whatever was going on. He doubted that Darnell would be rash enough to try to harm any of them in broad daylight. Not when he intended to have one of the guards go up to the mansion to fetch the lord of the manor.

First, Fargo intended to go on by and make a circuit of the property, to scout it out. But the sight of the gate hanging open and no one standing guard changed his mind. "Hold up," he called out, and once the team stopped, he jumped down and walked a few yards past the gate to scan the neatly tended lawn.

There was no sign of life. No gunmen patrolled the grounds. No one appeared at any of the windows.

"Wait here," Fargo directed and followed the drive to the portico. Quiet reigned, except for sparrows chirping in the roses and a dove cooing in a willow. Boldly, he stepped to the door and rapped, using the heavy brass knocker.

Within resounded a hollow echo. Fargo pressed an ear to the panel, but heard no footsteps, no outcries, nothing. He rapped again. When the same thing occurred, he tried the door and was not surprised to find it unlocked.

The interior was lavishly decorated and furnished. Standing on carpet over an inch thick, Fargo cupped a hand to his mouth. "Is anyone home?"

The shout echoed in the cavernous residence. Fargo checked the nearest rooms. They were empty save for the furniture. It was obvious that Darnell and his henchmen had cleared out. But why? Had Darnell been afraid that the law would show up on his doorstep?

A sound outside brought Fargo around in a crouch, his hand falling to his pistol. A shadow flitted across the doorway, then the person who cast it stepped into the mansion.

"See here! Who are you, sir? And what are you doing?" demanded a white-haired woman in her fifties or sixties, who wore a long dress and a bonnet. In her hand was a ring that held a number of large keys.

"I was looking for Mr. Darnell," Fargo said.

"Oh. I'm afraid you've just missed him," the woman said, relaxing and smiling. "He sent word early this morning that he was leaving sooner than he expected. Mighty strange, considering he leased the estate for a month and only stayed a few days. But I warned him up front that the money could not be refunded." A chatterbox, she chuckled and added, "I guess a man as rich as he is can afford to treat a thousand dollars as if it were small change."

Fargo made no attempt to hide his disappointment that Darnell was not there. "Who are you?"

"Jessica Walters. Six months out of the year I lease the estate for the owners, who go to Europe."

"Do you have any idea where Mr. Darnell went? It's important that I talk to him."

Walters shook her head. "I wish I could help you, young man. Tharon Darnell is a secretive man." She moved out onto the porch and Fargo tagged along. "My guess would be that he went back to St. Louis. That's where he has most of his extensive business holdings."

"So he lives in St. Louis?" Fargo found the news extremely interesting.

"Didn't you know that? Why, Tharon Lucien Darnell is a living legend in these parts. He's richer than Midas, or so folks claim. Got his start as a fire tender on a riverboat and worked his way up to become the head of a vast financial empire."

Inspiration prompted Fargo to ask, "Is he married, that you know?"

"Not that I heard tell. But a handsome man like him could have his pick of any young woman he wanted. He'd be the catch of the century." Walters tittered. "Why, if I were forty years younger, I might try to land him myself."

Fargo thanked her and headed for the gate. He knew more than he did before, but it only added to the mystery. What would a man like Tharon Darnell want with Amanda Templeton? Why had Darnell left Jefferson City without her, if she was so important to him that he sent four of his men to bring her back no matter what it took? None of it made any sense.

Mortimer J. Forbush did not like being kept waiting. "Enough of this nonsense, Mr. Fargo. Why did you keep us here cooling our heels? What is this all about?"

"I wanted to have you meet an acquaintance of mine," Fargo said as he climbed into the phaeton. "Tharon Darnell."

Forbush glanced at the mansion, worry contorting his face. Mandy did the same, only she was more terrified than worried. Both tried to hide it when Fargo looked at them, but they failed dismally.

"Tharon Darnell!" Bethany Cole exclaimed and clapped her hands. "Now I remember where I heard the name before. He's one of the richest men in St. Louis. The newspapers carry stories about him all the time."

Fargo held off asking about the kind of stories until he had given the coachman instructions to drive them to their hotel.

"Most have to do with his business dealings," Bethany said. "He owns riverboats, a shipping line, and a printing operation. He has homes in St. Louis, Philadelphia, and Chicago. I think he also has a ranch somewhere in Kansas. It's hard to keep track of it all."

Riverboats. A ranch. A shipping line. It explained why so many different kinds of men worked for Darnell, but not why he chose to surround himself with cutthroats who would gladly commit murder at his bidding, or whatever else he required of them.

An ethical businessman had no cause to hire killers. So Tharon Lucien Darnell must not be the financial knight in shining armor that the newspapers made him out to be. Hadn't Bethany just said that he owned a printing operation? Maybe, Fargo mused, Darnell had the stories written up himself.

To say that there was much more here than met the eye was the understatement of the century.

"When do you intend to leave for St. Louis?" Forbush wanted to learn.

"That depends on whether you want to take the stage or ride," Fargo said.

"You're actually giving us a choice?" Forbush grumbled. "My, aren't you feeling generous."

Mandy was seated next to him and had been paying close attention. Perking up, she said, "I love to ride on stages, Pa. Can we go on the next one out? Please?"

Fargo was going to agree when Mortimer suddenly

straightened and said, "No, let's ride. I tend to get sick on long stage runs."

"Darn it, Mortimer," Mandy said, upset until Forbush turned to her and mouthed a few words that only she could see. Mandy's eyes flicked to Fargo and back again. "All right," she said with great reluctance. "If it will make you sick, it's best we go on horseback. I like to ride almost as much as I like taking stagecoaches."

It didn't matter to Fargo much one way or the other. But he had to wonder what Forbush was up to, and why Amanda was so willing to agree to whatever Mortimer proposed. They were hiding something. The question was, what? And how should he go about discovering it, short of giving Forbush a beating to make him talk?

Bethany was speaking. "If we ride, we'll need to buy or rent horses. Who's going to pay for them? And what about a pack horse? It will take us four or five days to get there. We'll need enough supplies to see us through."

"I'll foot the bill," Mortimer readily offered. Much too readily, in Fargo's opinion.

"We'll need the rest of the day to prepare," Bethany said. "The earliest we can leave is tomorrow morning."

"Fine by me," Mortimer said cheerily. All of a sudden he was as happy as a lark, and he stayed that way even after they reached the hotel. Staying in his seat, he said, "I'll go straight to the nearest livery and arrange everything. Miss Cole, would you be so kind as to watch over Amanda while I'm gone?"

"I'd be glad to," Bethany said. "We can go shopping for items we'll need."

Mortimer gestured at the coachman and the phaeton rattled off. Fargo was inclined to follow it, but Mandy tugged on the whangs on his right sleeve.

"Want to come with us, Pa? We haven't had much time to ourselves. It will be terrific." When Fargo hesitated, she grabbed his hand in both of hers and started to pull him down the street. "Please!" she pleaded loudly, making such a spectacle of herself that passersby stopped to stare. "Miss Cole won't mind, will you, Miss Cole?"

"Not at all," Bethany said with an unusual little smile. "It will give us an opportunity to become better acquainted."

Fargo could think of any number of things he would rather do than go shopping with a pair of females, but he heard himself saying, "For you, Mandy, I'll do it."

"Oh, Pa!" the girl squealed and hugged his legs with so much enthusiasm that Fargo nearly tripped. Bethany laughed lightly, pried the child off, and each of them clasped one of his hands.

Not having ever been married, and since he seldom stayed with any one woman for more than a few weeks, Fargo had been spared ordeals that husbands knew all too well. From many a married man, over a shared bottle of whiskey, he had heard horror tales about peculiar female traits that made most men want to tear their hair out by the roots in exasperation.

Shopping was one of them. And on this day, Fargo learned the truth of what he had been told. Where he would have gone into a clothing store knowing what he wanted, buy it, and leave right away, Bethany had to try on every dress or blouse or shoe in the place and then agonize over which one fit the best. Where he would have gone into a general store and bought his supplies as quickly as possible, Bethany had to compare prices and brands and even *ingredients*.

Evidently it was a trait that females picked up at an early age because Mandy took just as long as Bethany to make up her mind.

Strangely enough, although Fargo did nothing but tag along, by three in the afternoon when they meandered toward the hotel, he felt as tired as if he had just run two miles over rough terrain.

Mortimer Forbush did not show up until five. Happier than ever, he treated Fargo and the others to supper. By seven Bethany and Mandy had turned in. Mortimer drifted off, so Fargo went to check on the Ovaro. Deep in thought, he had no idea that he was being followed until he drew abreast of an alley. Suddenly, heavy boots pounded behind him. Before he could turn, his arms were grabbed by two men. A foot caught him across the shins and he was thrown into the alley, sprawling on his belly. He tasted dirt and smelled the rank odor of refuse.

One of his attackers snickered. "Which leg should we break first?"

6

Skye Fargo rolled onto his back and tried to push to his feet, but a ponderous foot slammed into the pit of his gut, pinning him to the ground, even as a hand the size of a grizzly's paw snatched his Colt and flung it away. Above him reared a living mountain in shabby clothes, a colossus with bushy, beetling brows and small, dark beady eyes. Alcohol tinged his breath, and the top of a flask jutted from a pants pocket.

Fargo had seen the man's like many times before—men who spent every day and most of every night frequenting saloons; men who worked only when they had to; men who liked to guzzle until they were giddy; men who were fond of breaking skulls and busting bones and who loved to boast of it later.

The man's companion was cut from the same coarse cloth. Only a bit smaller than the one who had Fargo pinned, his chin was adorned by a bushy, unkempt beard. His thick nose was bent in the middle, the result of a break that had never mended properly. Clenching his oversized hands, he cracked his bony knuckles together and lumbered around Fargo like a shaggy bull buffalo.

"So this is the feller everyone jabbers about all the time?" the bruiser said. "The highfalutin Trailsman?" He grinned, exposing a gap where three of his upper front teeth had been. "He don't look like so much to me, Clem."

"Downright puny, if you ask me," Clem said, bending. His thick fingers grasped the front of Fargo's shirt. "Yellow, too, Hiram. See how he just lies here, quakin' in his boots."

"I don't see what that feller who hired us was so worried about," Hiram remarked. "Be real careful! he told us. As tough as an Apache! he claimed. Ha! This joker ain't no tougher than my nephew. And he's in diapers!"

"Ain't that the truth," Clem said, beginning to pull Fargo up. "Well, let's earn our pay. I'll do the ribs and you can stomp his arms and legs."

Fargo had let them prattle on. Dull wits made for loose lips, and now he had learned that someone paid them to cripple him. Who? Tharon Darnell? It was unlikely that a man with a small army of seasoned killers at his beck and call would rely on a pair of local lunkheads to do his dirty work.

"Any last words, Trailsman?" Clem goaded him, cocking his massive arm.

"I do have a question," Fargo said, still making no effort to defend himself. He wanted them to think he was cowed. He wanted them to think he wouldn't lift a finger against them.

"A question?" Clem repeated and winked at Hiram. "Ain't that the dumbest thing you ever heard?" Sneering at Fargo, he said, "Go ahead, puny feller. What do you want to know?"

"Did you ever plan on having kids?" Fargo asked, and as he uttered the last syllable, his right knee drove up and in, slamming into the living mountain's groin, driving his knee so far in, he could have sworn that it brushed the bruiser's spine.

For a second nothing happened. Then Clem darkened, his eyes bulged, his mouth fell open, and his fingers went limp. Mewing like a kitten, he gasped for breath, squeaking, "Damn you! Get him, Hiram!"

Fargo uncoiled, swinging his right arm straight up, his hand flat. The heel of his palm connected with Clem's lower jaw, crunching Clem's teeth together. Instantly, he pivoted and crouched.

Hiram's fist swished the air over Fargo's head. Sidestepping, Fargo kicked, ramming his boot into Hiram's left knee. There was a crack, and Hiram grimaced. Fargo waded in with both fists flying, raining them on the bigger man's face and neck, battering Hiram against the wall.

"Damn you!" Hiram raged, swinging his own arms in vain. Most of his blows cleaved thin air. "Clem, lend a hand here! He's liable to get away!"

But Fargo had no intention of running off. Blocking a left cross, he arched into an uppercut that rocked Hiram on his heels. As he drew back his right fist to follow through, he was seized from behind by arms as big as tree trunks and lifted bodily off the ground.

"I'm goin' to crush you like a bug!" Clem snarled in Fargo's ears. The twin pythons he called arms constricted, and acute anguish appeared through Fargo's chest. It felt as if every rib was on the verge of splintering.

Momentarily, Fargo's vision spun. Shaking his head to clear it, he whipped his head forward, then snapped it back again, into Clem's face. Cartilage crackled. Warm sticky drops spattered Fargo's neck. Clem roared like an enraged mountain lion and hurled Fargo down.

"My nose!" the hulking brute fumed, holding a brawny hand over it, blood pulsing between his fingers. "You broke my damn nose!"

Hiram advanced, limping. "Let me finish him for you, partner. I'll make this jasper wish he was never born."

Fargo twisted, curled his knee to his chest, then lanced them at Hiram's shins. It knocked Hiram clean off his feet. But instead of falling backward, Hiram pitched forward. Fargo scrambled aside, a fist clipping him on the shoulder. He was on his feet first, and he drew back a leg to kick Hiram on the jaw.

From out of nowhere hurtled a two-legged battering ram. Clem's left shoulder caught Fargo across the midsection, sweeping him off his feet as Clem's arms clamped around the small of Fargo's back.

"I'm goin' to break your spine!" the colossus growled, the lower half of his face a dark smear. Snorting, he applied more pressure, the bulging muscles on his arms rippling with raw power.

Sheer torment knifed up Fargo's backbone to jangle his senses. He fought down a rising scream. Seldom had he felt such pain! He pushed against Clem's chest, but it was like pushing against a brick wall. He punched Clem twice on the chin, but it was the same as striking an anvil. Demons danced in Clem's beady eyes, the demons of vengeance and blood lust.

"Break him, partner!" Hiram urged, rising slowly.

Fargo writhed, barely able to concentrate. The agony was excruciating. Pinpoints of bright light flickered before his eyes like a swarm of fireflies. Marshaling his strength, he hit the bruiser on the cheek, on the temple, on the eyebrow. He might as well have pounded on a stump for all the good it did him.

Feral glee lit Clem's brutish features. Teeth clenched, spittle dribbling from his mouth, he cackled harshly and exclaimed, "Can you feel it, boy? Feel your spine about to go?"

The trouble was, Fargo *could* feel it. His backbone was close to breaking. All the blood in his body seemed to have rushed to his head, rendering him sluggish. His tongue felt swollen, his lips puffy. He was like a balloon about to burst. In desperation he clawed at Clem's eyes, gouging his fingers in deep. Clem howled and attempted to shake Fargo's hands off, but Fargo gouged his nails in deeper.

Venting a wild animal cry of baffled fury, Clem threw Fargo from him. Fargo staggered, yet managed to stay on his feet. No sooner did he set himself than Hiram pounced, lunging at him with arms outflung, seeking to get him in the same spine-crunching grip Clem had used. Only this time Fargo was not caught flat-footed. Dancing under

Hiram's arm, he wheeled and smashed two swift blows to the kidneys. Hiram spun, but Fargo was faster. His leg forked Hiram's, and he shoved, sending the brawler into the wall headfirst.

Swearing lividly, Hiram reeled upright. His forehead was split, blood flowing into his eyes. "Damn you!" he bellowed, blinking to clear them. "Clem! Help me!"

Before the colossus could come to his friend's aid, Fargo slipped in close, tensed every sinew, and unleashed a right cross with all his power and weight behind it. The *crack* of his knuckles connecting with Hiram's chin was like a muffled gunshot. Consciousness fled, and Hiram buckled.

Fargo turned just as Clem came at him again. Eyes watering, Clem had to squint to see. He held his enormous fists at chest height, saying, "You're all mine now, puny man! This time I won't let you lay a finger on me."

True to his word, Clem flicked a combination that narrowly missed. His arms were much longer than Fargo's, and his greater reach was an asset he exploited. Circling to the left, he swung punch after punch.

A commotion at the alley mouth alerted Fargo to gathering bystanders. Any one of them might see fit to go fetch the marshal. He had to end the fight, and end it quickly. As he briskly stepped to the right to keep out of Clem's reach, he spotted his Colt a few yards off. Abruptly turning his back to the man-mountain, he lunged and scooped it up.

Roaring, Clem leaped. He must have figured that Fargo was running off, because he opened his arms wide as if intending to tackle Fargo before Fargo got much farther. Which played right into Fargo's hands.

Spinning, the Trailsman brought the barrel of his Colt crashing down on the crown of Clem's thick noggin. It slowed the bruiser, but did not stop him. Again Fargo struck, as Clem's arms closed. He thought that he hit the man hard enough to split a rail, but Clem kept on coming, plowing into him and bearing him to the dirt. Fargo shoved and wrenched, expecting Clem to battle fiercely. But the mountain lay strangely limp.

Shoving out from under the man's considerable bulk, Fargo stood. He would have liked to question the pair. Already, though, eight or nine people had gathered, and more were dashing across the street. He ran out, the onlookers parting to let him pass. No one had the temerity to try and stop him, not after what they had witnessed.

Bearing to the left at the next corner, Fargo slid the Colt into its scabbard. He covered two blocks, checking behind him frequently. As best he could determine, he was not being followed. Satisfied, he took a roundabout route to the livery.

Fargo did not stay long. After telling the proprietor that he would be leaving the next morning, he fed the Ovaro some oats and spent a little time stroking its neck and getting a burr out of its mane that he had missed when he arrived.

No one accosted him on his way to the Excelsior. Fargo was half a block away when he saw Mortimer J. Forbush emerge, glance furtively around as if to ensure he was not being watched, then hasten down the steps and hurry westward.

Suspicious, Fargo decided to learn where the lawyer was off to. Falling into step behind a knot of townsmen, he dogged Forbush to another hotel, the Imperial. Instead of entering, Mortimer sat down on a bench on the porch. He acted as nervous as a mouse in a barn full of cats, constantly glancing every which way, and fidgeting.

From a corner of a millinery, Fargo watched the entrance. He had a hunch that Forbush was there to meet someone, and he had a hunch who that person was. Tharon Lucien Darnell.

It made sense. Forbush had been acting secretive since Fargo met him, leading Fargo to suspect that the big secret was the fact Forbush and Darnell were in cahoots. Why, he could not say. To what end, he did not know. But someone had let Darnell know that Fargo was Amanda's alleged father, or Darnell would not have sent Jessie and those others to jump Fargo in his room.

Fargo would be the first to admit his reasoning was flawed. If Forbush was in league with Darnell, why hadn't the lawyer told Darnell that Mandy was staying with Bethany Cole, not Fargo?

Someone stepped from the Imperial. Forbush rose, snatched off his bowler, and gave a sort of bow. It was just the sort of thing Fargo would expect a coyote like Forbush to do when meeting a man of Darnell's stature. Only it wasn't Tharon Darnell. A *woman* had emerged, clad in a long dress and a cloak with a hood that covered her entire head and hid her face. She moved to the bench.

Fargo was stumped. It wasn't Bethany Cole. That much was obvious based on her body alone, which was more amply endowed than the schoolmarm's. She also had longer legs. He hoped the woman would pull back the hood so he could see her clearly, but she didn't.

They talked in whispers, huddled close. Forbush was upset. He gesticulated to accent his points and twice stamped his foot. The woman listened passively. When he had spent himself, she answered quietly and calmly. His response changed her demeanor. Sweeping erect, she pointed a finger at him and said something that made Forbush cringe as if lashed by a whip.

Fargo just had to find out who she was. But the moment he stepped into the open, she spotted him, whirled, and darted into the Imperial, her cloak swirling about her.

Forbush had not seen Fargo. He stood, perplexed by her sudden departure. Clasping his ever-present valise, Mortimer moved toward the entrance and wound up blocking the doorway at the very instant Fargo reached it.

"Out of the way," Fargo hollered, pushing the law wrangler aside. The spacious lobby of the Imperial was almost as richly furnished as that of the Excelsior. An elderly couple reading newspapers looked up, startled, as he barreled in. A nattily dressed man on a sofa frowned at his breach of good manners. And the desk clerk, a portly man with a balding pate that shone in the lamplight like a great gleaming egg, appeared none too pleased.

Of the woman in the hood, there was no trace. Fargo ran to the front desk. "Where did she go?"

"Who might that be, sir?" the clerk responded glibly.

"You know damn well who," Fargo said. "The lady in the cloak who came in right before I did. She must have gone up the stairs. Which room is she in?"

The man adjusted his spectacles and straightened his string tie. "I have no idea to whom you are referring, sir. And I must say, I resent how you have disturbed our guests. Not to mention your tone."

Fargo came close to seizing the clerk by the throat and shaking him until his spectacles fell off. "One last time. What room is she in?"

Puffing out his cheeks, the clerk snapped, "Are you here to take a room?"

"No. I want to—"

The clerk indicated the door. "Then I'll thank you to leave or I'll send for the marshal to have you thrown out."

"I just need to know who she is," Fargo tried to be reasonable. He glanced at the register.

Slamming it shut, the clerk shoved the gold-embossed book under the counter. "The Imperial does not disclose the names of its guests to every scruffy character who strays in off the street. For the last time, no woman answering that description is staying here. Go. Now. Or else."

Everyone else was staring. A bellboy had appeared from somewhere and hovered near the front desk, eager to be off to fetch the law should the clerk give the word.

Recognizing a lost cause when he saw one, Fargo tromped from the lobby. Forbush was gone. Which figured. He moved out into the street and scanned the windows above. Silhouetted behind the lacy curtain of one on the third floor was a woman in a cloak. She cracked the curtain to stare down at him, her face shrouded by her hood.

Fargo touched his hat brim, then left. Learning her identity was not worth a clash with the law. At the Excelsior, he was passing the dining room when he saw Mortimer Forbush sipping coffee. Veering over to the table, he leaned on it and demanded, "Who was she?"

Acting as innocent as a lamb, Mortimer set down his cup and said, "I beg your pardon? Whom are you referring to?"

Fargo's patience snapped. Like a striking rattler his hand darted out and closed on the lawyer's windpipe. "I'm tired of being played for a fool. What are you up to, Forbush?"

Mortimer struggled to pry Fargo's fingers apart, but he was as helpless as a prairie dog in the grip of a wolf. Sputtering, he grew red in the face and would have swooned had Fargo not relaxed his fingers.

"Well?"

"How dare you!" Forbush huffed. Gulping water, he composed himself enough to say, "My personal affairs are none of your concern. But I will let you know that the woman you saw me with is a long-time acquaintance of mine. We're quite close, if you get my meaning. Or we were."

Could it be? Fargo wondered. Or was the lawyer doing what lawyers always did when caught doing something they shouldn't do, namely, lying through his teeth?

"It upsets me greatly that you've been spying on me," Forbush went on. "How would *you* take it if I had the nerve to do the same to you?"

"If what you say is true, why did your lady friend run off when she saw me?"

"She ran off because we'd had an argument and she was in tears. She doesn't even know you."

Fargo couldn't see any woman crying over Mortimer Forbush, but stranger things had happened. It was entirely possible that he had just made a royal jackass of himself. Disgusted both at the lawyer and his own temper, he marched from the dining room and started up the stairs, nearly colliding with Bethany Cole.

"Oh! Skye! I had no idea you were back," the schoolmarm said and read his expression. "What's wrong? Why do you look as if you'd like to throttle someone?"

"Lawyers!" Fargo spat. He did not go into detail. "Where's Mandy?" he asked, worried that the girl was not with Cole. Since Darnell was gone, the child should be safe enough alone. Then again, it was hard to believe that a man like Tharon Darnell would easily give up on anyone or anything.

"Asleep in our room, the poor dear," Bethany said. "I don't think she slept well last night. She was tired all day. Shopping wore her out even more."

Fargo saw no need to mention that Amanda had been fatigued because she stayed up so late waiting for him the night before. "Did you lock the door?"

"What do you take me for? Certainly," Bethany said. She patted the handbag that hung from her shoulder. "I have the key right here. She's safe enough."

"Good." Fargo started to go on, but the schoolmarm grasped his hand. Her fingers were warm, her palm as soft as silk. Something about her touch stirred his loins.

"Hold on. Haven't you wondered why I took your side this morning? Why I voted to go to St. Louis to locate people who knew Rosalie Templeton?" Bethany looked up and down the stairs, verifying no one was close enough to overhear. "It's because I think something is dreadfully wrong. And I'd like to help you get to the bottom of it."

This was a switch, Fargo reflected. Not twenty-four hours ago she had treated him as if he were the worst polecat alive. Now she was anxious to lend a hand? "What did I do to change your mind about me?" he bluntly asked.

"You didn't do a thing. Mandy did." Bethany sidled closer to whisper, which put the swell of her bosom less than an inch from his chest and her full cherry lips so close to his that he had a near irresistible urge to plant his mouth on hers. "Something is terribly wrong with that girl."

"So you noticed, too."

Bethany did not seem to move, yet her lips were now almost brushing his, her mint-scented breath tingling his nose. "I can't put my finger on any one thing she's said or done. It's more like all of them combined have given me the impression that she is hiding something. But I haven't the slightest idea what it might be."

"Still think I'm her father?"

"I honestly can't say. If you're not, it's her bad luck. You'd make a fine one, I believe, if you ever put your mind to it."

Fargo nudged her. "Were my ears playing tricks on me? Or did you just pay me a compliment?"

Bethany laughed and unconsciously reached up to stroke his cheek. "I'm mature enough to admit when I'm wrong, and I was wrong about you. You do care for Mandy. I saw it in your eyes today when she was dragging you all over the place. Deep down, you have a heart of gold."

"Don't tell anyone. I don't want to ruin my reputation."

They both laughed, and Bethany's hand strayed to his shoulder and rested there as if it were the most natural thing in the world for her to do. Catching herself, she stood back and bowed her head, embarrassed. "Maybe we can talk about this more some other time?"

"Whenever you want," Fargo said. She smiled and continued down the stairs, unaware that his gaze trailed her. The enticing sway of her hips stimulated him, reminding him of how many days it had been since last he shared his bed. Sighing, he put such romantic notions from his mind. Schoolmarms were notoriously prim and upstanding. It would scandalize a woman like Bethany if she were privy to his innermost thoughts.

Fargo climbed to his room. He had learned his lesson last night, so when he opened the door this time, he did so with one hand on his Colt, and he did not go in until he was confident the room was empty. Lighting the lamp, he unbuckled his gunbelt and placed it on the bed.

They had agreed to leave at eight the next morning. He had to be up long before that to get the Ovaro and buy cartridges for his rifle, which he had neglected to do earlier.

Fargo washed his face and was lifting his shirt to strip it off when someone knocked. Pulling the pistol out, he moved to the jamb. "Who is it?"

No one answered.

Gripping the latch, Fargo yanked the door wide and extended the Colt. Discovering who it was startled him as much as he startled her.

Mustering a timid smile, Bethany Cole walked past him and sat on the edge of his bed. "Mind if we have that talk now?"

7

"I was just washing up," Skye Fargo said. Peeling off his buckskin shirt, he stepped to the basin. The position of the washstand enabled him to see the bed out of the corner of his eye, and he noticed that the schoolmarm ran her eyes over his chest and back, then rimmed her red lips with the pink tip of her tongue. Inwardly, he smiled.

"Don't let me stop you," Bethany Cole said more huskily than Fargo had ever heard her say anything. She coughed as if to clear her throat and asked, "Have you seen how Mortimer and Mandy whisper to each other all the time?"

"They're right friendly," Fargo said, dipping the washcloth into the basin.

"What do you make of it?"

"You tell me." Fargo began wiping his chest. Her hooded smoldering eyes were mesmerized by his every motion. When he lifted an arm to do his ribs, her mouth formed a luscious little oval. At length she found her voice.

"Either they have a secret they don't want us to know, or they're up to something."

"One leads to the other," Fargo said, twisting so his back was reflected in the mirror on the wall. He could see the schoolmarm without her being aware. As he washed, she crossed and uncrossed her long legs.

"What do you intend to do?"

"Life is a lot like poker. Sometimes you have to let the other players show their hands before you can show yours. Mortimer and Mandy have to make the first move."

Bethany grinned warmly. "How philosophical. You are constantly surprising me, one way or another."

"I hope they're pleasant surprises," Fargo baited her and was rewarded with a faint blush. "I wouldn't want you to think poorly of me."

"Oh, no. Never."

Done with the cloth, Fargo hung it on the small ring provided and stepped to the chair, swinging it around so that he could straddle it facing the bed. "I should warn you, Miss Cole—"

"Call me Bethany, please," she demurely insisted.

"Bethany," Fargo said suggestively, openly admiring the rhythmic rise and fall of her bosom. Distracted, he forgot what he was going to say and she had to remind him.

"What's this about a warning?"

"There is more involved here than you know," Fargo said. "It could be dangerous for you to tag along with us."

"Surely you're exaggerating."

"Last night I was jumped by four men in this very room. Men who wanted to get their hands on Mandy. Today, two men tried to beat the tar out of me. It's all tied together, somehow."

"Goodness gracious! They beat you?" Impulsively, Bethany rose and touched the left side of his forehead. "Is that how you got this bruise?"

Nodding, Fargo gently clasped her hand and lowered it to a spot on his shoulder where one of Clem's punches had clipped him. "And this welt," he said.

Bethany lightly ran a fingertip over it and shivered as if cold. "Why do they want Mandy?" she inquired, her voice oddly strained.

"Your guess is as good as mine." Fargo slowly rose, took her hand, and roamed her palm lower, across his shoulder to his chest. "That feels good," he said. "Maybe I can persuade you to give me a back rub." His hand drew hers lower, to the hard muscles that lined his abdomen.

It was the moment of truth. Either she would bolt like a

frightened doe, or she had in mind what he thought she had in mind.

Bethany's lower lip quivered as she roved her hand over his muscles. A hungry look came over her, a look that had no relation to food or drink. Drawing back her arm, she said softly, "I think I should leave."

"Don't go on my account," Fargo said. Making no sudden moves, he grasped both her wrists and raised her hands to his chest again. She swallowed, then massaged him in ever widening circles.

"This isn't right. It isn't why I came," Bethany said.

They both knew she was denying the truth, but Fargo was not about to hurt her feelings by pointing it out. Taking her right wrist, he gambled everything on a brazen tactic. He lowered her hand to his rigid manhood.

Bethany stiffened and gasped. Fear and passion fought for dominance in her eyes. She began to step back, but stopped. Holding her breath, she curled her fingers around his pole and cooed thickly, "It's so big!"

"It gets bigger. Would you like to see?" Swiftly, Fargo unhitched his pants and lowered them just enough for his engorged pole to jut out. Bethany's eyes widened. She offered no resistance when he placed her hand on it. As it grew, she swayed, and for a moment there he thought that she was going to faint. "Are you all right?"

Her response was to fling herself into his arms and mold her lusting lips to his. An inner dam had burst, releasing feelings she had pent up probably her entire life. Her velvet tongue glided between his teeth. Her full body mashed against his, the swell of her breasts increasing as she rubbed herself against him like a human match trying to build enough friction between them so she could burst into flame.

Fargo walked her toward the bed, a small step at a time. He rubbed her back, her shoulders, her neck. She sucked on his tongue, her nails biting into his arms, the intensity of her desire so acute it was painful. Panting, she broke the kiss and fixed him with fiery pools of volcanic carnal abandon. Gone was the prim and proper schoolmarm. In her place stood a wanton woman in all her sensual glory.

"I want you."

"No fooling?" Fargo quipped, but the jest was lost on her. She had one thing in mind and one thing alone. Gripping his cheeks, she pulled his face down to hers. He brought both hands around and with no forewarning covered her breasts.

"Ohhhhhh," Bethany moaned as Fargo squeezed and tweaked them. She wriggled against him, her thighs sliding against one another. When he found a hardening nipple and lightly pinched it between a thumb and forefinger, she arched her back and stifled a low outcry.

Easing her onto the bed, Fargo stretched out beside her. All pretense had evaporated. Her leg crooked, her dress sliding clear down to her marble thigh, but she made no attempt to cover herself. A nail, hooking under his chin, drew their lips together again. And if he thought her kisses had been fiery before, they paled in comparison to the ones she gave him now. She was an inferno unleashed, boiling over with raw erotic cravings.

Fargo unfastened her dress, taking his sweet time. To rush would spoil a special night she would remember for the rest of her life. Prying at hooks and clasps and buttons, he exposed her underthings. Another few seconds, and her glorious globes burst their bounds, her tawny nipples thrusting upward like twin tiny spikes. He covered one with his mouth, savoring the delicious taste and the scent of perfume strategically placed.

"Ahhhhh! I love it!" Bethany breathed.

Lathering her breasts, Fargo dipped his other hand to her belly, which trembled at his touch. Her hips were thrusting against his in instinctive anticipation of what was to come. Kneading her flesh, Fargo sucked a luscious nipple into his mouth and rolled it with his tongue as he might a ripe grape. Her knee parted his legs to stroke his inner thigh, inflaming his manhood to new heights.

Slipping a hand under her dress, Fargo swirled his fingers nearer and nearer to her nether mound. He brushed crinkly hair and plucked at it, eliciting a mew of delight. His forefinger traveled lower, to her nether lips, which were moist and wanting. When he brushed them, she shook as if having a convulsion, her breasts quaking under his mouth.

"Oh! Oh! I never—!"

Ever so tenderly, Fargo inserted the tip of his finger. Her fingernails raked his back, and he knew she had drawn blood. Undaunted, he eased his finger in deeper, a fraction at a time. Her inner walls throbbed with rampant need. They clung to his finger, and yet yielded to it, simultaneously. At last he sank it in to the knuckle.

Bethany held her breath, realizing what he would do next. At his first stroke, she lurched upward as if to bear him off the bed. Her head thrashed and wordless sounds issued from her throat. She was so excited that her eyelids fluttered and she inhaled raggedly. "Wonderful!" she mouthed. "Marvelous!"

Fargo was just getting started. He adopted a steady in-and-out pumping motion. Her bottom scooted up and down in a matching tempo.

Some women were always nervous about making love— as if afraid they would do it wrong. Yet when they let themselves go, when they let passion rule, their bodies took over and did what came naturally. They had no cause to fret.

Bethany became more animated. Her hands roamed through Fargo's hair and along his shoulders to his arms, raising goosebumps with her scraping nails. Her thighs widened so he could slip between them, but he was not quite ready for the final act in their coupling, so he held off. He did insert another finger into her slick tunnel. It made her bite her lower lip and whimper in ecstasy.

Bethany's mouth locked onto his. She gave him a kiss that he felt clear down to his toes. Her right hand, caressing his side, moved lower, crossing his hip to grasp his member. Unexpected, it sent electric ripples through Fargo's body. His pulsing organ threatened to explode.

Not yet! Fargo willed. Every ounce of self-control he possessed had to be called on to keep him from erupting prematurely. She rubbed him, then cupped his stalk and massaged his pods. Now it was his turn to shiver, to groan deep in his chest.

Hastily, Fargo removed the rest of her clothes. His own, as well. Naked, they lay nose to nose, exploring one another with lips and hands. He reveled in the silken sheen of her skin and could tell that she was equally enamored of his finely molded sinews.

"So different, so fine," Bethany whispered in confirmation.

Rolling her onto her back, Fargo lay between her legs, his organ lying across her mound, giving her a foretaste of what was next. She shifted and lifted, trying to impale him, but he deftly twisted, avoiding her to prolong their mutual release. Cupping both breasts, he kneaded them as if they were bread dough. Bethany's hand drifted to his buttocks, giving them the same treatment.

Tongues entwined, they rocked up and down to an inner beat only they could hear. Or rather, feel. Internally, tom-toms pounded in rising volume and urgency. Their temples thrummed, their blood hummed. They were lost to the world, adrift in a sea of physical senses, lost to everything around them, conscious only of one another and their growing need.

This was the moment Fargo lived for. Of all life's many pleasures, this was the very best. Of all the experiences known to mortal man, none matched the joining of a man and woman. It was the pinnacle of existence, a rapture so exquisite that it was intoxicating. Let other men be addicted to alcohol or opium or cards or horse racing, or any of the thousand and one pursuits of the human race. *This* was what thrilled Fargo more than anything else. *This* was what put zest into his life, what invigorated his soul.

Suddenly, Fargo realized that Bethany had shifted again. Before he could react, her sheath swallowed his sword. Her walls constricted, holding him there. Up his back shot sensations of pure bliss.

"Now! Please! Now!"

Her appeal did not fall on deaf ears. Gripping her hips for leverage, Fargo rose onto his knees. She forked her legs behind his back, locking her ankles. At his first plunge, she cried out. At his second, she grasped his shoulders and threw back her head.

From then on their union was a blur of rocking bodies, of burning lips and feverish fingers, of scorched flesh and shared breath. Piercing, soothing, as sweet as sugar, all softness and angles. Presently, the bubbling center of her core gushed in a tremor of release, a tremor so strong, it bounced the bed on which they lay.

"Yessssssss! I'm there!" Bethany said, clutching him close, her face against his shoulder, her smooth thighs bonding to hold him in place. "I'm commmmmiiinnnnngg!"

Fargo felt her spurt. He rode her until she sank back, exhausted, then he rammed into her harder than ever. Surprise opened her eyes. "You didn't—?" she said, and moaned long and loud. Her body once more rose to meet his. Their thrusts were wild, reckless, primitive. A knot formed at the base of Fargo's spine, a knot that expanded, that shot through him like a red-hot knife. He could not have held back any longer if his life depended on it.

He exploded. And as he did, she did. This time it was better than the first. This time she kicked and tossed and stifled a scream that would have awakened everyone in the hotel.

When it was over, Fargo coasted to a stop, slid onto his side, and breathed deeply. Sweat caked every square inch.

He was limp and tired. His eyelids weighed tons. Closing them, he drifted off.

How long Fargo slept, he could not say, at first. A sound brought him out of a slumber so deep that he was loath to wake up. Beside him Bethany snored lightly. He assumed she was to blame and went to go back to sleep when an odd rasping noise fell on his ears. Flogging his weary brain, he raised his head—and saw the latch move. Someone was in the hall!

Fargo could not recollect if he had locked the door or not. Slipping to the end of the bed, he palmed the Colt and rose. The latch stopped moving when he was halfway across. Whoever was out there had learned that the door was indeed bolted.

Not caring that he had no clothes on, Fargo quietly slid the bolt back, gripped the latch, and tensed. Yanking the door wide, he leveled his Colt. Only no one was there. He bounded into the corridor, swiveling from right to left. It was empty and still.

But that couldn't be! Whoever had tried the latch had not had enough time to reach the stairway to the lobby or the rear stairs. Where else could they have gone? Fargo wondered. Into another room?

Retreating into his own, Fargo dressed, strapped on his gunbelt, and left again. He moved rapidly toward Bethany's room, anxious to confirm Amanda was all right. Their door was closed, but he tested it to be sure. About to leave, he put an ear to the wood.

Inside, someone was whispering. Mandy, he believed. She stopped, and he strained to hear the voice of the person in there with her, but no one spoke. Then Mandy whispered again, as if answering. He could not make out what she was saying although he did catch the name, "Mortimer."

Fargo drew back a fist to knock. They would let him in, or else. Then he heard Mandy say clearly, "Look out! Someone is coming down the street!"

Insight spurred Fargo into racing to the rear stairs. He

bounded down three at a stride, slowing near the bottom. Careful not to make noise, he cracked the door and peered out. A horse and rider were going by, the man whistling softly. Judging by his clothes, he was a farmer on his way home. As soon as the horse vanished in the darkness, a tall figure in a hooded cloak came from the shadows at the corner of the hotel and moved to a point where Bethany Cole's window was visible.

Fargo opened the door a little further. It was the mystery woman from the Imperial, the one who had met Mortimer J. Forbush. Now she was here, in the middle of the night, talking to Amanda. What in the world was going on?

"I'd better go now," the woman whispered. The hood concealed all but the tip of her nose. Her voice was deep and sultry, the kind that quickened a man's pulse just to hear it.

"I wish you would come up," Mandy replied.

"You know better. We have to play this out to the end, child. Trust me. It's the only way."

"It stinks," Mandy whispered flatly. "I wish he were dead! He deserves it, for what he did."

The woman lifted a shapely hand in a touching gesture of farewell. "Be strong, child. Be brave. Come what may, always remember how it was. And try not to judge him too harshly. He can no more help the way he is than a gator can. He deserves our pity, not our hate."

"He's a pig," Amanda said.

Without thinking, Fargo looked up. Was Mandy referring to him? Was that how she truly felt? He turned back to the mystery woman. She had seen him! Spinning, her cloak swirling about her, she bolted, fleeing down the street with astounding speed. Shoving the door open, Fargo gave chase. He glanced back once at Mandy's window, but she was gone.

Knuckling down, Fargo ran for all he was worth. In his youth he had won many a foot race. And while he was not the fleetest man alive, neither was he a slouch. He could outdistance almost anyone, given time.

The woman, though, was bound and determined not to be caught. A human antelope, she bounded along at a clip that few could match. That included Fargo. He was hard pressed not to lose ground. Several times she looked at him, her hood sliding higher but not high enough to afford him a clear image of her face.

People were abroad, but not many. A few hollered for Fargo to stop. One man even pursued him for several blocks, shouting, "Stop, you! Let that woman be!"

Fargo figured his quarry would head for the Imperial. He was wrong. Five blocks from the Excelsior she took a left fork that soon brought her to a section of the town where lamps were few and far between. She knew Jefferson City much better than he did. Whether it would prove enough to enable her to elude him remained to be seen.

Her speed, her lithe economy of movement, reminded Fargo of a Sioux maiden he had met when he was barely old enough to shave. A maiden who could outrun any man, white or red. He had been smitten with her, but she had eyes only for the most stalwart warrior in her tribe.

The woman in the cloak darted into a narrow space between two rows of small shacks. Home to Jefferson City's poorest, each was no bigger than Fargo's room at the Excelsior, yet might be home for a family of nine or ten. Most were dark, since few who lived there could afford lanterns or even candles.

Fargo followed her. A solid wall of inky blackness enveloped him. He could not see his hand at arm's length, let alone the mystery woman. The patter of her flying feet guided him. Then the patter abruptly died.

Instantly, Fargo stopped. Had she sped around one of the shacks? Or was she ahead somewhere, stock-still, hoping to throw him off her scent by not moving? He listened, but heard only the wail of an infant in the distance and a man coughing nearby. Crouching, he tried to spot her profile silhouetted against the background of stars, but it did not work.

Seconds ticked by with unbearable slowness. Fargo inched forward, probing every nook and cranny. Suddenly, the door to the third shack on the right opened, framing a stocky man in a nightshirt who held a candle. "I'll be right back—" he was saying to someone, then was rooted in place at sight of the supple figure caught in his candle's feeble glare.

The woman's hood was down. Like a tawny cougar she pivoted and ran. Fargo glimpsed a face as lovely as the schoolmarm's, hair the color of golden straw. He sprinted past the man in the nightshirt.

"Hey! What the hell is going on?"

The mystery woman glided to the right, between two shacks and into an open field. It was the first mistake she had made, and Fargo smiled. He had her now. The waist-high grass whipped around his legs as he churned in her wake. She was no more than thirty feet in front of him when she angled to the left and dropped from sight. Just like that. Fargo reached the exact area in seconds, but she was gone.

Fargo crouched, thinking she was on her hands and knees, tunneling through the grass. But his ears detected no sound other than the whisper of the wind, the croak of tree frogs, and the drone of insects.

She was trying the same trick again. For a while Fargo bided his time. When she did not move, he did, circling in an ever wider pattern, making no more noise than would a fox or bobcat.

He did not find her. Frustrated, he zigzagged back and forth from one end of the field to the other. He scared off two rabbits. He sent a mouse or rat scurrying away. He shied from a large snake that hissed and coiled. But he did not locate the woman in the cloak.

She had done what few others ever could. She had shaken him off her trail as handily as he had given countless others the slip. Instead of being annoyed, he found himself admiring her even more. It took a woman with rare talent to beat him at what he was best at.

Fargo bent his steps toward the hotel. At the edge of the field he paused to scan it one last time. "You're a sly one," he said aloud. And as if in response, the cool breeze fanned his face, bringing with it the faint merry tinkle of feminine laughter.

8

Skye Fargo was ready to leave Jefferson City by seven the next morning, but it was almost nine before they departed. The problem was Mandy. She refused to leave her room. Bethany spent nearly two hours trying to talk the girl into it, and finally they came out, Mandy with her head high, her chin jutting defiantly at the world. She gave Forbush a crisp "Good morning." But she did not say a word to Fargo. Nor would she so much as look at him, even after they were mounted and winding out of town. Whenever Fargo twisted in the saddle to look back, she averted her face.

Bethany Cole kneed her mare alongside the pinto. "What is that all about?" she asked with a nod at the child.

Fargo had not told anyone else about his encounter with the lady in the cloak. When he had returned to his room, Bethany had been gone, leaving a short note to explain that she had woke up and hurried back to her own room in case Amanda awakened and found her missing. Little did Bethany know that Mandy had been awake the whole time, talking to the mystery woman.

"Skye?" Bethany prompted when Fargo said nothing.

"Sorry," Fargo said. "I didn't get much sleep last night."

Bethany's contented smile was downright devilish. "Do tell. You're not the only one." She snickered and leaned toward him. "If I'd had any idea what it was going to be like, I wouldn't have taken so long to get up my courage and pay you that visit."

Fargo chuckled. Nine times out of ten, once a woman's

prim and proper reserve melted away, she turned into a passionate wildcat. The schoolmarm promised to be no different.

"What about Mandy?" Bethany asked again. "Do you have any idea why she's treating you like dirt?"

"Maybe I can find out," Fargo hedged and slowed until the girl was even with him. "Morning," he said.

Amanda gazed straight ahead, her small jaw locked.

"You can't ignore me the whole trip," Fargo said. "Sooner or later you'll have to talk to me."

"Go away."

Fargo let a minute go by before he tried again. "I take it that you're mad because of last night. But I'm the one who should be upset with you. It's not right to keep secrets from your pa. Who was that woman you were talking to?"

Mandy swiveled, spite contorting her features. She was so mad, she was beet red. Stabbing a finger at him, she said, "You had no business chasing her off like you did!"

"I only wanted to find out who she was," Fargo calmly responded. "I never meant her any harm. But she wouldn't let me get close to her. She got away."

"She did?" Mandy blinked, then smiled slyly. "And you're supposed to be so good at tracking and catching people! I guess you're not as great as the newspapers claim, Pa."

Fargo almost said something he would regret. He had to remind himself that she was a bitter, heartbroken child who had yet to come to terms with the loss of her mother. "Is she a relative? Or maybe a friend of your ma's?"

Pondering a bit, Mandy nodded and said, "All right. I'll tell you. She's a friend. But I won't say who she is, because she doesn't want me to tell anyone, and I gave my word that I wouldn't."

"Why doesn't she just come out in the open?"

"She has her reasons." With that, the girl goaded her pony a few yards forward, effectively putting an end to their conversation.

Fargo did not press it. If and when the child decided to talk, she would. No amount of persuasion could force her to. Twisting in the saddle, he regarded the lawyer, who had hardly spoken five times all morning. Forbush was in a sullen funk, plodding awkwardly along on a roan, leading their pack horse. The trail behind them was clear.

Assuming the lead again, Fargo did not stop until the sun was directly overhead. In a clearing that bordered the road he drew rein and announced they would rest for half an hour. Had he been by himself, he would have gone on until sunset. But Mandy was drowsy, and Forbush was having a hard time sitting still.

Dismounting, Fargo loosened the cinch on his saddle and let the stallion graze as it pleased. Under a spreading oak he sat with his back to the trunk. The schoolmarm was giving Amanda water from the water skin they had brought along. Mortimer J. Forbush had climbed stiffly down and was pacing and flexing his legs.

"We haven't been on the road a whole day yet, and I'm so sore I can barely stand it," the lawyer complained. "By tonight I'll probably have so many blisters, I won't be able to sit down."

"You don't do much riding, do you, Mr. Forbush?" Bethany Cole asked.

"I *never* ride if I can help it," Mortimer said. "Why bother, when a carriage can take you anywhere in much more comfort?" He scowled at the roan. "Besides, horses are such smelly, sweaty beasts. I don't see how anyone can stand to be around them."

Fargo paused in the act of idly plucking blades of grass. It struck him as peculiar that Forbush detested horses and riding, when it had been the lawyer who suggested they ride to St. Louis in the first place. It made more sense for Forbush to want to rent a carriage or take the stage. Dismissing it as a quirk, he commented, "Think of how the horse feels."

"What do you mean?"

"You're one of the worst riders I've ever seen." Fargo did not mince words. "You flop around on that roan's back like a fish out of water. You jerk on the reins when you shouldn't, and you're always banging your knees and legs against him. It's a wonder he hasn't thrown you by now."

"Hmmmmph!" Forbush snorted and walked off in a huff, kicking at stones and twigs in his path.

Frowning, Fargo pulled his hat brim low against the sun. It was going to be a *long* trek to St. Louis. Between the threat posed by Darnell, the woman in the cloak, and his own companions, he would have his hands full. Closing his eyes, he tried to relax, to enjoy fifteen or twenty minutes of peace and quiet. He should not have bothered.

Footsteps approached. "I think it's time we got to know each other better, Pa," Amanda Templeton announced, taking a seat beside him.

Fargo folded his arms and said, "Can't we do it later? I'd like to take a nap."

"You'd rather sleep than spend time with me, your own flesh and blood?" Mandy said, her shock transparent. "What kind of man are you, anyhow?"

"The kind who never counted on having kids," Fargo noted. Since she was not going to go away until she was good and ready, he sat up and glanced at her. "What do you want to know about me?"

Questions poured from the girl like water from the spout of a well pump. "Things like, what's your favorite food? Do you have any other kin? Why do you wander all over the place? What do you like to do most? Is it true you once killed six Apaches at one time? How late will you let me stay up at night, nine or maybe ten?"

"Six," Fargo answered the last one. "A girl your age has no business being up to all hours."

"Goodness, you're stricter than Ma," Mandy said.

"What was she like?" Fargo quizzed.

A dreamy look came over the girl. "Oh, she was the nicest, sweetest mother anyone could have. She liked to bake cakes and tell me stories and take me for long walks in the woods. She taught me how to draw and paint and took me to a museum once to see paintings by famous artists. And we would go to music shows sometimes and the county fair every summer."

"What did she look like?"

Amanda stared at a yellow butterfly flitting by. "She had black hair and brown eyes."

Fargo figured Mandy would say more, but the child simply watched the butterfly alight on a flower. "What else can you tell me about her?"

"That's all," Mandy said stiffly and rose. "I guess I'll stretch my legs a while. See you." Whistling, she skipped off, as happy as a lark.

Her mood swings puzzled Fargo. Was her mother's death to blame? Or had Amanda always been this way? He watched her chase the butterfly, laughing in childish abandon. It was one of the few times he had seen her act her age. Little by little she was coming out of her shell. Given time, she might even open fully to him and tell him everything he needed to know.

Fargo leaned back. There was still time to rest. Then a shadow fell across him and musky perfume competed with the scent of the flowers.

"Well, I see the two of you are on friendly terms again," Bethany said, sliding down beside him. "That's a good sign. If anyone can help her recover from her loss, it's you."

The schoolmarm had bought a special outfit for their journey. A form-hugging white blouse accented her upper charms, while a tight pair of smooth leather pants molded to her legs like a second skin. Watching her move was enough to bring a lump to Fargo's throat. "Why wouldn't Mandy leave her room this morning?"

"She would never say," Bethany answered. "All she did was sit in a chair, staring out a window at the street behind the hotel."

At where the mystery woman had been, Fargo guessed. It would be best if he told the schoolmarm what happened, but just then a screech of mortal terror shattered the stillness. He sprang erect, rotating as Mortimer J. Forbush barreled from the undergrowth wildly flapping both of his spindly arms.

"Help! Help me!"

"What's wrong?" Fargo demanded, scouring the growth for enemies.

"A bee!" Forbush cried. "A huge bee is trying to sting me!" He danced and hopped and skipped and yelped, in a perfect panic. "Don't just stand there, damn you! Do something!"

Fargo had seen the offending insect. Regretting that he had not insisted they take the stage, he grabbed the lawyer as Forbush pranced past. "Calm down. It's just a fly."

"A what?" Mortimer said, cringing and glancing fearfully at the black dot buzzing above him.

"A fly," Fargo repeated. He gave it a swat that whisked it into a stand of high weeds.

"Really?" Mortimer slowly lowered his arms. "But I've never seen one that big before. Anyone could have made the same mistake."

Not anyone with half a brain, Fargo was tempted to say, but he didn't. Bethany had risen and gone to Mandy, so he walked to the pack horse and helped himself to a handful of jerky. Moving to the road, he gazed westward. An elderly man on a mule plodded along hundreds of yards away. Shifting eastward, he saw a wagon laden with farm produce.

All morning they had passed fellow travelers going in both directions. Most had been ordinary people going about their daily lives. Once, a hawk-faced man in a suit and wide-brimmed black hat had ridden by. A gambler, Fargo suspected. Another time it had been a weary army patrol, the captain in command doffing his hat to the schoolmarm and Amanda.

Presently, Fargo called to the others and climbed on the stallion. He gave each of them a piece of jerky, took the reins to the packhorse himself, and rode out at a brisk walk. At the rate they were going, it would take them a week to reach St. Louis unless they picked up the pace.

By the middle of the afternoon Forbush was clinging to his saddle horn and groaning every now and then. During a fifteen-minute break Fargo called at three, he folded a blanket and draped it over his saddle, but the added cushioning did not lessen his discomfort once they were under way.

Amanda was in fine spirits. She sang. She hummed. She pointed out clouds in the shape of horses and chickens and cats and such.

Bethany spent most of her time with Mandy. Which was fine by Fargo. He had a lot to reflect on. Too many pieces to the puzzle were missing for him to reach any firm conclusions, but he did decide that the woman in the cloak was the key to solving the mystery. She knew Mandy. She knew Forbush. She had known Rosalie Templeton. Odds were, then, that she could tell him what the others were hiding.

Twilight found them on the crest of a low hill. Fargo had picked the spot because he could see for miles around. A small stream gurgled past the site. While he took the horses to drink, Bethany and Amanda started a fire. Mortimer gathered wood.

They had brought enough canned goods and the like to last for five days. Fargo would have preferred fresh roasted meat, but he had no complaints with the stew the schoolmarm made. It was delicious. Dipping in a hot roll, he ate like a famished wolf.

Everyone was hungry except Forbush. He could not bear to sit for any length of time. Over and over he whined like a stricken puppy. It got to the point where Fargo took their container of butter, grabbed the lawyer by the arm, and dragged him into the brush. "Here. Rub it where your hurt the most. Try not to use it all."

"You're proposing that I use this?" Mortimer sputtered,

waving the container. "Are you serious? I'll be all . . . squishy."

"Would you rather be in pain?" Shaking his head, Fargo returned to the fire and added a few small dead branches. Mandy was curled up under her blankets, close to drifting off. Bethany had produced a book and was reading by the firelight. "Keep an eye on things," he directed her. "I'll be back in a while."

Henry in hand, Fargo ventured partway down the slope to a gigantic maple. A magnificent tree, it sported half a dozen low, wide branches. Onto one of them he clambered, straddling the limb and bracing himself against the trunk. From his vantage point he marked the pale ribbon of road as it wound through the wilderness. Approximately a mile off gleamed an orange ball of light. A campfire. Another glimmered two miles away on a lower hill.

Innocent travelers? Or someone trailing them? Fargo would have gone to find out, but he was reluctant to leave Bethany and Mandy alone. Forbush would be next to useless if they were attacked. Truth was, they'd probably have to protect *him*.

Fargo remained in his roost for half an hour. He counted two more fires, so far in the distance they were pinpoints of flickering light. As he rose to swing down, he saw a third, a land-bound star on the horizon. Considering how heavily used the road between St. Louis and Jefferson City was, the number did not seem high.

Even so, Fargo took precautions. Once back at camp, he lined up his saddle, his saddlebags, and the rest of his effects in a row, added a few short branches, and spread out a blanket, arranging it so that anyone lurking in the forest would think he was sound asleep, his head resting on his saddle.

No one asked him what he was up to. Mortimer had done as he suggested, but kept on moaning and fidgeting. Bethany read. Mandy, exhausted, slept the deep sleep of the innocent, her brow as smooth as glass.

"I'll be nearby in case you need me," Fargo assured the schoolmarm.

Bethany looked up. The firelight played over the cover of her book, which showed outlandishly dressed frontiersmen and ridiculously garbed warriors in heated battle around a scantily clad Indian maiden. The title said it all. *Maleska: The Indian Wife of the White Hunter.* "You must expect trouble."

"If anyone does pay us a visit, they'll regret it," Fargo vowed.

Mortimer moaned. "I just hope all this trouble we're going to is worth it. My posterior is so sore I'm liable to faint if I have to answer nature's call."

"Please, Mr. Forbush!" Bethany said. "I haven't ridden in almost a year, but you don't hear me complaining."

"Only because men and women aren't built the same," Mortimer said. "Everyone knows that women have softer, more ample bottoms. For you, sitting a saddle is like resting on pillows."

Bethany lowered her dime novel. "That's enough out of you, sir! The comment you just made is the stupidest I have ever heard, and doesn't merit a reply."

Fargo had to walk off before he broke out laughing and woke up Mandy. Forbush was amazing. The man knew as little about females as he did about everything else. Taking up a position behind a log that rimmed the clearing on the north, Fargo folded the blanket he had brought, then spread out on it.

The fire crackled and sparked. Bethany stayed up another hour reading, then turned in. Mortimer tried to sleep, but could not lie still for long, and every time he rolled onto his back, he would wake up with a start. Toward midnight he thought to lay on his side with his back against his saddle so he could not roll over, and finally fell asleep.

Fargo gazed at the myriad of stars, feeling drowsy himself. A soft breeze rustled the trees. Crickets chirped noisily off in the forest. To the south a coyote yipped and was answered by another to the west. And, of course, an owl voiced the eternal question of its kind.

The familiar sounds lulled Fargo into drifting off. By habit a light sleeper, he came awake immediately when his senses detected something was wrong. It wasn't a specific noise that woke him up. It was the *silence*. All the crickets had stopped chirping. In fact, every last insect had fallen quiet. It might be a sign that a predator was on the prowl. And the predator could be four-legged—or two-legged.

Rising on an elbow, Fargo scanned the tree line. If something or someone was out there, they were lying low. He tucked the stock of the Henry to his shoulder, just in case.

So far as Fargo knew, the last grizzly had been killed in Missouri some time ago. Black bears were abundant, but they seldom bothered humans. Cougars were plentiful, yet the same applied to them. Wolves would attack when rabid or ravenous, but he had not heard a single plaintive howl all night.

Fargo remembered the stories he had heard about roving bands of Northern and Southern sympathizers. Marauders, many of them, using the conflict as an excuse to murder, rape, and pillage. Usually they did not venture this close to Jefferson City, but there was a first time for everything.

Then he saw them—figures moving back among the trees. He spotted two, but there might be more. Taking a hasty bead, he touched his finger to the trigger. But the target he had picked moved behind a trunk, foiling him. He swung the barrel toward the second figure, but it also disappeared.

Damn! Fargo mentally swore. The pair had separated. They appeared to be moving toward the camp from opposite directions. Lowering the Henry, he snaked toward an earthen mound twenty feet away. From on top of it he would have a clear shot at anything that stepped into the firelight on either side of the clearing.

To the northwest a twig snapped. Then weeds shook

loudly. One of the men was as stealthy as a drunk with blinders on.

Fargo hurried to reach the mound before they were in position. One of the horses nickered, and at that the woods fell quiet again. He crawled to the crest. Slowly, he rose onto his knees.

For the longest while the only sound was the crackle of the fire. Fargo hoped they would close in before the flames died out. In the dark a stray bullet might well hit the schoolmarm or Mandy. If a slug should hit the lawyer—well, the world had too many lawyers, as it was.

A huge form reared beside an oak across the clearing. Fargo shifted and took aim. At that range he could not miss. But he held off, wanting the man to take one more step so he could see who it was. So intent was he on the huge figure that he was a split second too late in reacting to a muffled tread behind him.

A mallet slammed into Fargo's head. Or so it seemed, as a tidal wave of pain swamped him and a black veil descended. He barely felt his body strike the ground. Vaguely, he knew the Henry had been torn from his grasp and someone was fumbling at his holster. Struggling not to succumb to the veil, he pushed at the hand and was buffeted across the cheek. Iron fingers gripped him by the back of the shirt. Something scraped his face as he was dragged down the mound.

A sinister chuckle gnawed at Fargo's consciousness. It reminded him that Bethany and Mandy were in danger, that they had depended on him and he had let them down. With a supreme effort of sheer willpower, he cast the veil from his mind just as he was kicked in the ribs and sent tumbling toward the fire. He stopped shy of the flames, his chest in agony.

"What in the hell?" That was Mortimer J. Forbush, sitting and gaping at the pair of giants who loomed out of the encircling night. He pulled his blanket up to his chin as if to hide from them. "What do you want?"

Mandy sat, took one look, screamed, and scooted over to Bethany Cole, who was blinking sleep from her eyes. Rising onto one knee, the schoolmarm draped an arm over the girl's shoulder and fearlessly demanded, "Who are you? What is the meaning of this outrage?"

"Shut up, woman!" snarled the larger of the pair, shaking a callused fist. "If you know what's good for you, you'll only talk when we say to talk." Bending until his battered, bruised, and swollen face was inches from Fargo's, he gripped Fargo's shirt. "Remember us, mister?"

How could Fargo forget. It was Clem—with Hiram. And they weren't there to pay a social call.

9

"On your feet!" Clem snarled. The colossus viciously yanked Skye Fargo upright. Automatically, Fargo cocked his arm, but as he went to swing, he saw Hiram pointing a rifle at Bethany Cole and Mandy.

"No, you don't!" the second bruiser warned. "Lift a finger against us and this pretty lady will suffer."

Clem smirked in triumph. "It's our turn now, bastard. We couldn't wait to pay you back for the stompin' you gave us. When we heard tell that you'd left town with this bunch, we jumped on our mules and lit a shuck." He shook Fargo, reveling in the power they had over him. "Now we get to do what we were paid to do."

"Speakin' of which," Hiram said, nodding at Mortimer J. Forbush, "take a gander at the law wrangler, sittin' there as white as a sheet and actin' like he don't know us from Adam."

Clem chortled. "What's the matter, Morty? Cat got your tongue? Or are you just afraid to own up to what you done, with these other folks standin' here?"

Forbush had to try twice before he could make his tongue work. "I have no idea what you are talking about, gentlemen," he squeaked.

Clem let go of Fargo to slap his massive thigh. "Ain't he a caution, pard? He paid us all that money to bust the Trailsman's bones, but he don't have the gumption to admit it." The walking mountain kicked dirt at the lawyer and

swore. "Pitiful! That's what you are, Morty. The most pitiful excuse for a man I ever did see."

Bethany had risen and stepped in front of Mandy to
protect her. Appalled by the revelation, she exclaimed,
"Mortimer! What got into you? Why would you do such a
thing?"

Forbush was quaking like a leaf in a gale. "I don't know
what these men are talking about, Miss Cole," he said
through chattering teeth. "I never hired them to harm anyone. They are both lying."

"What?" Clem thundered, then was on the lawyer before
Mortimer could blink. Seizing him by the throat, Clem
hoisted Forbush into the air. "Call us liars, will you? I
should strangle you for the insult." Throwing Mortimer
down hard, he slammed a foot onto the lawyer's stomach.
Forbush screeched and clasped himself.

Hiram took one hand off his rifle to reach into a pocket
and pull out a leather poke. Jingling the coins it held, he
said, "Hear that, missy? It's my half of the money that no-
account polecat claims he didn't pay us. Fifty dollars
each, it was. Just to fix the Trailsman so he couldn't go
nowhere."

For the moment, the pair had forgotten about Fargo.
Sidling to the left half a stride, he tensed his legs and balled
his right hand at his side.

Clem stomped on Forbush again and Mortimer curled
into a ball, whining pitiably. " 'Course," Clem said, "you
told us it had to be done before you rode out. We tried to do
as you wanted, but he's tricky, that coon is." Straightening,
he smacked his right fist into his left palm. "Now we owe
him personal-like. No one licks us and gets to brag on it."

"Sure enough," Hiram agreed, starting to slide the poke
back into his pocket. "So let's get to it. And remember,
partner, you break all his bones from the waist up. I get to
break all of 'em from the waist down. Don't you get carried
away, like you always do."

Fargo's moment of truth had come. Uncoiling, he drove

his fist into Hiram's jaw, and the man crashed to the ground like a poled ox. Fargo pivoted to confront Clem, but he was not halfway around when Clem's enormous arms looped his chest and hoisted him off his feet.

"This is where we left off, puny feller!"

It was, and Fargo did the same thing he had done the last time to break free. He snapped his head forward, then back, to smash Clem in the face. But Clem had learned. The colossus jerked his face aside and laughed.

"You'll have to come up with somethin' new, mister! I'm not as dumb as most think. I never fall for the same trick twice!"

The arms banding Fargo's chest constricted, exerting incredible pressure. Fargo felt as if his rib cage were caving in. Agony speared through him, and the clearing spun before his eyes. When it stopped spinning, he saw Bethany rushing toward them with a jagged rock in her upraised hand.

"No! Stop hurting him!"

Clem grunted when the rock smashed into his temple. Stunned, he wobbled backward, shaking his bull head and bellowing, "Hiram! Get up, damn you! This female is tryin' to brain me!"

Bethany sprang again, swinging the bloody rock in an arc that caught Clem flush on the cheek and ruptured it like a ripe melon.

Howling, Clem skipped to one side, refusing to relinquish his hold on Fargo, his arms continuing to constrict all the while.

Fargo writhed in torment. Punching the arms had no effect. So, frantic, he bent his neck and bit down on Clem's wrist, shearing his teeth through flesh and sinew. Blood spurted onto his lips and tongue.

Roaring like a beast gone mad, Clem flung Fargo from him and pressed his wrist to his side. "He bit me, Hiram! The son of a bitch *bit* me!"

Hiram was rising. He lunged, catching Bethany's wrist as she drew her arm back to hit Clem again.

Fargo leaped to the schoolmarm's rescue. Hiram was about to punch her when he dived, ramming his shoulder into Hiram's stomach and folding Hiram like an accordion. Grappling, they crashed to the ground. Hiram, on top, rained his fists on Fargo's head and shoulders.

"I've got you now, puny feller!"

At that there was a sharp retort, the crack of a small-caliber gun, and a tiny hole blossomed in the center of Hiram's forehead. A look of dumb amazement came over him. Arms drooping, he wilted like a dead plant.

Fargo shoved the man's bulk off and surged onto his hands and knees. He glanced at Bethany, then Mortimer, but neither held a pistol. Turning, he was as dumfounded as they were to see Mandy with a smoking derringer in her hand.

"I couldn't let him hurt you," the girl said softly.

Clem was riveted to his friend's fallen form. "Nooooo!" he suddenly bawled. "You little witch! I'll kill you for that!" Spinning toward Amanda, he clawed at his revolver.

The rifle that Hiram had dropped lay a few feet from Fargo. He threw himself at it, snatching the Sharps on the fly and rolling on his shoulder. Rising into a crouch, he tucked the stock against his side and swung the barrel until it pointed at Clem. The colossus was just bringing the revolver to bear. Fargo's thumb worked, his finger squeezed. The heavy .44-90 boomed like a cannon, the recoil thrusting the stock rearward.

At that range the impact was like the kick of a Missouri mule. Clem was struck in the sternum, lifted clear off his feet, and hurled four or five feet to sprawl onto his back with his limbs flopping. He still held his pistol.

Fargo's own Colt was wedged under Clem's belt. Dropping the single-shot Sharps, he drew the Arkansas tooth-pick from his right boot and darted forward.

Clem's eyes were rolling in his head, his face ashen.

From the hole in his chest gushed his lifeblood. He was trying to say something, but no words came out. Gradually, his arms flopped less and less. His revolver slipped from his fingers. A final breath was expelled from his lungs.

Fargo claimed his Colt, then replaced his knife. He went to Mandy and pried the .41-caliber derringer from her limp hand. It was the smallest derringer made, easily concealed, with little kick.

Mandy was in shock, gaping blankly at Hiram. "I killed him," she said, practically whispering. "I just wanted him to stop hurting you, and I killed him."

Kneeling, Fargo reached out to comfort her. Suddenly, she was in his arms, holding him close, a torrent of tears unleashed. Self-consciously, he hugged her. Her small frame racked with sobs for the longest while. She cried herself out on his broad shoulder, then stepped back, sniffling. A study in misery, she looked at him in mute appeal.

What should he say? Fargo asked himself. That she had crossed a line no one should ever have to cross? That if she let it eat at her, she would never know peace for as long as she lived? No. That would never do. "There's no need to fret. You did what you thought was right."

"Will I go to Hell?" Mandy asked.

"What?"

"Ma used to read to me from the Good Book a lot. One of the Ten Commandments is that we shall not kill. Remember?" Mandy wiped a sleeve across her nose. "Does this mean I won't go to Heaven?"

Fargo was at a loss to know what to say. He had never read the Bible clean through, and the few times he had gone to church, the sermons had bored him to death. But he was not about to say anything to shatter the child's faith. Just as he respected Indian beliefs about the hereafter, so did he respect those whites who were sincere about their religion. He just wasn't ready to take any of it seriously himself.

Bethany spared him from having to answer. "No, dear,

you won't go to Hell," she told the girl. "God knows why you did what you did."

Moving like a sleepwalker, Mandy walked to the schoolmarm and they embraced.

Fargo slowly rose. His gaze fell on Mortimer J. Forbush, who was sitting up. A red haze flared before him, and taking a single bound, he backhanded the lawyer across the face. Mortimer was knocked onto his back, eyes wide with fright.

"This is all your fault!" Fargo declared, backhanding Forbush again as the man tried to get up. "Because of you, two men are dead!" He hit Forbush a third time. "Because of you, that poor girl is scarred for life!"

"Stop!" Mortimer screamed as Fargo elevated his hand again. "They were lying, I tell you! I never hired them to beat you up! You have to believe me!"

"Believe *you*!" Fargo said and grabbed Mortimer's throat, on the brink of venting his frustration and fury. A tiny hand on his arm stopped him.

"No, Pa," Mandy said. "Please don't. As a favor to me. He's not as bad as you think he is."

Fargo straightened, his emotions in a tangle. What did she mean by that? Why would she stand up for Forbush, after what the lawyer had done? "For you," he said. Backing off, he stabbed a finger at Mortimer, saying, "But you had better stay out of my way from here on out. The next time—" He left the threat unfinished. Putting a hand to his brow, he walked off to be by himself, to sort his thoughts and regain his self-control.

Somehow or other he ended up at the horses. Going to the Ovaro, he leaned against it and waited for his temples to quit pounding. He had never come so close to beating a defenseless man senseless before. It upset him terribly. This whole business was getting to him in ways that nothing else ever had.

Mandy was the reason. He had started to treat her as if she truly were his daughter. He was being as protective of her as any real father would be. And that was not right. It wasn't fair to him, and it wasn't fair to her. Until it was proven beyond a shadow of a doubt that she was his child, it was better for both of them if he kept his distance.

But it was growing harder to do. The more they were together, the more fond of her he grew, and the more he found himself wondering if he should simply accept her claim at face value and do what everyone else seemed to think he should.

"Are you all right, Skye?"

Fargo straightened. Bethany was at his elbow. She touched his arm, seeking her answer in his eyes. "I'm fine," he lied. "What about the others?"

"Mortimer is pouting, as usual. I made Mandy get back under her blankets and turn in. She'll cry herself to sleep, I would imagine. Which is the best thing for her, right now."

"Good." Fargo thought she would leave, but she looked at him as if expecting him to say something more. "I'd better drag those bodies off. It wouldn't do to leave them there for Mandy to see when she wakes up tomorrow."

"Sure. Of course," Bethany said, sounding disappointed.

The task was a herculean labor. Clem weighed in excess of three hundred pounds, while Hiram had to tip the scales at two hundred and seventy-five. Fargo spent twenty minutes alone dragging Clem fifty yards into the woods. He would pull and tug and heave until he was tired, then rest for a minute and start all over again. Hiram was easier to handle. Fargo could drape Hiram over his shoulders without getting blood all over himself.

After going through their pockets, Fargo scooped out shallow graves for each. He covered the dirt mounds with as many branches and rocks as he could find to deter scavengers.

Bethany, Mandy, and Mortimer were all slumbering when Fargo came out of the trees. He doused the fire, moved to his blanket behind the log, and was asleep himself seconds after his head touched the ground.

Morning dawned brisk and bright. The aroma of coffee brought Fargo around, and he rose, scolding himself for having overslept. Bethany was busy making breakfast. Amanda sat with her chin on her knees, her arms wrapped around her legs. She wore a vacant stare and only mumbled when Fargo greeted her. Mortimer had his back to the fire, ignoring everyone.

"You should have woke me up," Fargo said, accepting a hot cup of Arbuckle's.

"You needed to rest," Bethany smiled, stirring batter in a pan. "I'm hungry, but the rest say they aren't. What about you? How many flapjacks would you like?"

"Six will do since we want our grub to last. Thanks." Sitting by Mandy, he sipped his coffee and studied her without her suspecting that he was. "I counted on seeing you smile today."

The girl placed her forehead on her arm. "This isn't going anything like it should. We were never supposed to go back to St. Louis. Those men were not supposed to come after us."

"Things don't always work out like we want them to," Fargo mentioned. "That's just the way life is."

"But she said—" Mandy began, and stopped herself.

"Who said what?"

"Nothing. Forget it." The child was quiet for a spell. In due course she raised her troubled face to him and asked, out of the blue, "How many men have you killed?"

Fargo had often heard it claimed that kids came up with the darndest questions, but some of Mandy's threw him for a loop. This was one of them. "I don't keep count."

"Does it ever bother you?"

Choosing his words with care, Fargo replied, "I kill only when I'm left no choice. If it were up to me, I'd go through the rest of my life without ever shooting a soul. But that's not likely to happen. These are hard times, girl. Violent times. And there are a lot of violent people out there. White men who rob and murder just for the hell of it. Red men who kill to count coup on their enemies. Just to stay alive, I've had to defend myself against men like them from time to time. That's all there is to it."

Mandy was still not satisfied. "But does it *bother* you?"

"No," Fargo confessed and recalled the time a filly in Denver had dragged him to church one Sunday morning. That particular sermon was one of the few he recollected fairly well. "Remember Samson? He killed the enemies of his people, didn't he? He had to, or they would have killed him. It's the same with me. When I shoot someone, I do it because I have to. And it ends there. I don't have nightmares. I don't cry and moan. I get on with my life."

Soon breakfast was ready. Fargo accepted a plate from Bethany and made a big show of smacking his lips with each bite and making little sounds to show how much he was enjoying himself. It worked. Mandy could take only so much before she turned to the schoolmarm and said, "I've changed my mind, Miss Cole. If you don't mind, I'd like to eat."

By eight they were in the saddle. Fargo had located the two mules belonging to Clem and Hiram and used his lariat to link them and the packhorse in a string. He gave the end of the rope to Forbush, without comment, then rode eastward.

The brilliant sunshine, the crisp air, the chirping birds, they all brought Mandy out of her doldrums. By the middle of the morning she was as perky as a spry colt, joking with Bethany and laughing at the antics of a gray squirrel.

Fargo was at ease, too. The feeling that they were being followed was gone. He checked their back trail from time to time, but never saw any reason to be concerned. The people they passed were run-of-the-mill Missourians. For the first time in days, all seemed right with the world.

Mortimer kept to himself. During their noon rest, he moved off to sit under a pine.

"Excuse me," Mandy said and skipped over to him. They huddled a while, talking in low tones. At one point Mandy patted his hand, as if to bolster his spirits.

"Isn't she special?" Bethany said. "The way she cares for other people is just marvelous."

Fargo did not give voice to the doubt that ate at his insides like bitter acid. Nor did he bring up the issue uppermost in his mind until that evening, after the horses had been tended and while Bethany was fixing supper. Mandy strolled a little way down the road, fascinated by the colorful sunset. He came up behind her and said, "If you think this is something, you should see the sun go down behind the Rockies. It's too beautiful for me to describe."

The girl arched a brow. "I didn't think you noticed such things, Pa."

"I notice a lot of things," Fargo said, taking out the object he had kept in his pocket all day. "This derringer, for instance. Where did you get it?" He had not brought the subject up sooner for fear of upsetting her over Hiram's death. But it was time he found out.

"Ma gave it to me. She taught me how to load it and how to shoot straight."

Fargo hefted the tiny weapon, a favorite of gamblers and ladies of the night. "Why?"

Mandy shrugged. "She thought I might need it to protect myself."

"A girl your age? Who would want to harm you?"

Again Amanda shrugged. "There's no telling. Weren't you the one who told me this is a violent world? Ma wanted me to feel safe, is all."

Fargo did not believe that for a moment. No mother in her right mind would allow a girl so young to carry a loaded pistol unless there was a damn good reason. Unless the mother was certain the child's life was at risk. But who could Rosalie Templeton have thought would hurt her child? On a hunch, he asked, "What can you tell me about Tharon Darnell?"

Mandy turned toward the sunset. But she was not quick enough to hide the fleeting fear that flowered at the mention of the man's name. "I never heard of him before you brought him up the other day."

"You wouldn't be lying to me, would you?" Fargo asked. "No daughter of mine should ever tell a lie."

"Ma used to say the same thing," Amanda noted. She did not, however, answer the question. "Talk to you later," she said and danced off, singing a popular nursery rhyme.

Fargo let her go. It would be a waste of breath to try and convince her to talk. Whatever secret she was hiding, she hid it well. For one so little she was remarkably tight-lipped. Pocketing the derringer, he followed her back. The aroma of simmering beans made his mouth water.

The evening passed quietly. Across the road a family of five in a covered wagon stopped for the night. They had a girl about Mandy's age, and it wasn't long before the two were the best of friends, chatting and laughing and darting from camp to camp. Bethany had to call three times before Mandy came to turn in.

"Can't I spend the night with Melissa and her family? She's awful nice. I promise I'll behave."

"It's best if you stay with us," Bethany said.

"But I don't want to!" Mandy protested. Raising her voice, she said, "It's not fair. The first fun I've had in weeks, and you spoil it. I can go stay with them if I want to. You're not my mother. You can't make me do what you want."

"I can," Fargo interjected to end the tantrum. "As your guardian, it's up to me. And I say you stay here."

Mandy was so mad she stomped her feet. "You're not—" she said, then abruptly fell silent for a few seconds. "I mean, you haven't signed the papers yet. And you're not my guardian until you do."

Fargo looked to Mortimer for support, but the lawyer

would not even look at him. "It doesn't matter," he said. "You're not going back over, and that's all there is to it." With a start, he realized just how much like a parent he sounded. It was spooky.

For all her protests, Amanda fell asleep shortly after lying down. An hour later, it was Forbush's turn. By ten the only one still up was Fargo. The fire had dwindled to tiny fingers of flame, so, rising, he carried his blanket into the trees and spread it out. As he was setting the Henry on it, warm fingers brushed his neck.

"I couldn't sleep," Bethany said, tracing the outline of his jaw. "Want some company?"

"What did you have in mind?"

Despite the dark, the schoolmarm's eyes twinkled. "Three guesses."

10

Women never ceased to amaze Skye Fargo. Most would not let a man so much as touch them until they were well acquainted. A kiss was treated as a prize that the man must earn after a lot of courting. As for anything else, that involved even more effort. But once the man won the woman over, once most women had shared that first kiss and possibly bared their souls, they wanted more of the same. A lot more. And they had a knack for wanting it at the oddest times.

Take the schoolmarm, for instance. Here they were, not sixty feet from Mortimer and Amanda, in a country swarming with roving bands of marauders, with Tharon Darnell lurking in the background waiting to pounce—and Bethany Cole waxed romantic. Yet he was quite certain that if he had gone to her and given her hints that he wanted to traipse off into the trees, she would have turned him down, branding him as randy in the bargain.

There were times when Fargo secretly suspected that the sole purpose of women was to aggravate men.

Not that Fargo was going to object. The night was quiet. Mandy and the lawyer were sound asleep. And the family across the road, with their two dogs, was added insurance that no one could sneak up on them without being caught. "Aren't you a bundle of surprises," he said.

Bethany was flattered. Suggestively swaying her hips, she said, "I can't stop thinking of the other night. It was incredible."

"And you want a second helping," Fargo said matter-of-factly, running his gaze up and down her lush body. It was flawless. Rising, he took her hand and backed another dozen steps into the forest, into a grassy glade bathed by gentle starlight. With each step his hunger mounted. Her full bosom and the hint of silken thighs under her dress were more than enough to swell his manhood.

"I don't want to be gone too long," Bethany commented.

"You won't be," Fargo said huskily, hardly recognizing his own voice. Grasping her firm bottom, he yanked her forward, grinding his pole into her mound.

"Oh, my!" Bethany said, taken back by the urgency of his passion. "You must want me as much as I want you."

"You could say that," Fargo husked, lowering his mouth to hers. Greedily, he kissed her, parting her even teeth with his tongue. When her tongue jutted to meet his, he sucked hers into his mouth. At the same moment he kneaded her buttocks, parting them to slide a finger as far down as he could reach.

"My goodness!" she said when they broke for air. "You act as if you want to eat me alive!"

Fargo smiled. "Now there's an idea," he said, and before she quite knew what he was about, he had swooped her into his arms, spun in a circle, and lowered her to the grass.

"What—?" Bethany said, her eyes widening when he threw the hem of her dress up onto her knees and groped her underthings. "Already? I was—Ohhhhhh!"

Whatever else she was going to say was cut off by the contact of Fargo's lips and her inner thigh. Licking a path from just above her knee to within inches of her bushy triangle, Fargo parted her legs and settled onto his knees between them. He could hear her pant. The panting grew heavier and louder as he molded her warm flesh with his lips while moving ever so slowly toward the fount of her womanhood.

The musky scent of her core heightened Fargo's desire. His nose pressed against the silken material that covered her nether lips. She was hot and moist and quivering with anticipation. Moving the garment aside, he inserted his tongue, and at the first flick of her tiny knob, she bent her back and pressed her hand to her mouth.

"Ahhhhhhh! No one has ever done that before!"

Fargo was glad to be the first. Swirling his tongue, he gripped her thighs and indulged himself at length. Bethany began to lift her pert backside off the ground, pumping against him. Locking both lips onto her knob, he sucked as he might on a straw. It drove her into wild ecstasy. Her fingers clamped onto the back of his head and pushed as if she were striving to shove him up inside of her.

"Don't stop! Oh, don't ever stop!"

He did his best to oblige, but at length his tongue and jaw were so sore that he had to pull away. By then she was set and wanting and tossing her head from side to side in open abandon. She grabbed him by the shirt and pulled him to her.

"Please! Now!"

Fargo did not answer. But he was not ready yet. Working his hands up her dress, he cupped her heaving mounds and squeezed them harder than he ever had. It elicited a low moan. Kneading her ripe hard nipples between his thumb and a forefinger, he aroused her to a fever pitch. She slid her bottom against his legs to rub herself on his knee.

"I want you so much."

The feeling was mutual. Fargo lathered her neck, nibbled on an earlobe, then took the lobe between his lips. His breath fanned her ear and cheek. He saw her eyelids flutter. Slipping his right hand below her waist, he gauged the exact position of her tunnel and pierced it with his middle finger, burying the digit to the knuckle.

"Uhhhhh!" Bethany gasped. "Do me! Do me."

Fargo stroked his finger in and out, building the friction to the point where she thrashed under him and uttered deep lusty groans with each thrust. She was a volcano about to erupt, a dam about to burst. Unknown to her, he had slipped his gunbelt and pants down around his knees, freeing his straining pole. She did not guess his purpose when he rimmed her core, parting her nether lips.

"I want . . . I want . . ."

Bethany never said exactly what she wanted. For Fargo picked that moment to ram his organ into her with the force of a battering ram. It lifted her clear off the grass. She clung to him, her forehead against his chest, and voiced tiny gasps and coos, vibrant, on the brink of release. Fargo held onto her posterior, poised, savoring the sensation, drawing it out so their mutual pleasure would be that much greater.

"Please," Bethany said softly. "Please."

Rocking on his knees, Fargo began a pumping motion. There was nothing gentle about his lovemaking this time. He craved her as much as she craved him. His strokes were swift and strong, his urgency all-consuming. So powerful were his thrusts that she was rendered speechless with rapture, lost in lust as elemental as the wind, as chaotic as a storm.

Like a matched set of bookends, they were locked head to toe. One's motion complimented the other's. She met each stab with equal force, giving as good as she got, doing what she could to bring him to the summit so their release would be simultaneous. And while she was not as experienced as a saloon dove might be, her instincts were infallible. Her inner walls contracted in a tempo of their own. Her belly heaved, her breasts jiggled, her mouth was a furnace.

Fargo felt himself nearing the peak. To get her there first, he smothered her breasts with his lips. She heaved up against him, her fingers entwined in his hair, her other hand digging grooves in his back.

Suddenly, Bethany stiffened. Her mouth parted, and a silent scream issued out. Grasping him by the waist, she threw herself against him in savage need, her bottom bouncing and contracting and doing all those other things that drove a man over the edge. It worked. His explosion came mere seconds after hers. They pumped and pushed and pulsed, lost in the delirium of release. Had a tree fallen right next to them, they would not have noticed. If a wolf pack had surrounded them, they would not have cared. The exquisite sensation shooting through them was the sum total of who they were and all that was and ever had been and would ever be. It was the moment of moments, the one Fargo lived for, the one he could no more do without than he could do without breathing.

Spent, they coasted to a stop, Fargo lying on top of her, her damp hair against his temple. Easing off, he lay on his side and closed his eyes.

"That was great. Thank you," Bethany said, stroking his beaded brow.

"Any time," Fargo said softly. The tender caress of her fingers combined with the mild caress of the breeze lulled him into drifting off. He did not mean to sleep very long, but judging by the position of the stars when he opened his eyes, he had been out for over an hour. The schoolmarm was lost to the world, breathing deeply. He covered her breasts, lowered her dress, and sat up to don his pants and his gunbelt.

It was then, across the road, that one of the dogs barked. The other promptly joined in.

Jumping up, Fargo scanned the woods. Not seeing anyone, he judged it safe to let Bethany sleep for a while more. The dogs had fallen silent when he reached the clearing. Across the way, nothing moved.

Mandy snored lightly. Mortimer J. Forbush had his back propped against his saddle again and was mumbling in his sleep. Enough of the fire remained to reveal that the horses were dozing, even the Ovaro. After feeding a few small branches to the flames, he walked to the road and looked in both directions. It was empty.

There was no cause for alarm that Fargo could see. He figured that the dogs had barked at a passing raccoon or opossum or whatever. Checking the coffeepot, he found enough to fill a cup. He carried it past his blanket to the glade, intending to treat the schoolmarm.

Bethany Cole was gone.

Fargo surveyed the woodland. He did not spot her, but he was not overly worried. It seemed logical that she had awakened and gone off into the bushes. Kneeling, he yawned. He could use some coffee himself. After a minute had gone by, he gave in to temptation and enjoyed a sip. Then another.

"Bethany?" Fargo called out quietly so his voice would not carry as far as the clearing and disturb Amanda's slumber.

She did not answer.

Growing concerned, Fargo stood and paced the perimeter of the glade. "Bethany?" he repeated. "Where are you?" Still she did not respond. Mystified, he circled in a wider pattern. How could she have vanished? he asked himself. He had not been gone that long, and there had been no outcry. Nor was there evidence of a struggle.

No unusual noises rose from the depths of the forest. Nerves on edge, Fargo searched for over fifteen minutes, calling her name every so often. At last he had to admit the truth. The schoolmarm was gone.

Gulping the rest of the coffee, Fargo ran to his blanket. Once he had claimed the Henry, he hurried to the fire and selected a burning brand to be his makeshift torch. Amanda stirred, but she did not awaken.

All sorts of possibilities flashed through Fargo's mind as he raced back. A cougar had slunk out of the trees and bit Bethany on the neck, killing her instantly, then dragged the body off. Or marauders had been spying on the camp and carted her off, smothering her cries for help.

Yet if that was so, why had the grass not shown any sign to that effect?

The brand flickered and hissed as Fargo bent to examine the glade again. This time he saw details he had missed in the dark. Of special interest were bent blades, sign left by a lone man who had sneaked out of the bushes and over to where the schoolmarm had been lying. Whoever it was had been awful light on his feet, moving as an Indian would. The man must have knocked Bethany out because he had picked her up without protest, probably slinging her over a shoulder. The sign led off into the same bushes. From there the man had looped around to the east.

Fargo followed the tracks until the brand went out. The light lasted long enough to reveal that the culprit had secreted a mount over a hundred yards from their camp, near the road. Evidently the man had hoisted Bethany onto the back of the horse and ridden off.

In frustration, Fargo kicked a clod of dirt. The only thing to do was give chase, but how could he, when he had Mandy to think of? Leaving her behind with no one for company except Forbush was out of the question. Yet, taking her along would slow him down so badly that his chances of overtaking the schoolmarm's abductor were as slim as a fence rail. It was a case of damned if he did, and doubly damned if he didn't.

Fargo briefly considered leaving Mandy with the farm family. He hardly knew them well enough to impose, though, and if Darnell showed up, the entire family, sprouts and all, would be in danger.

No, as much as Fargo hated to admit it, he couldn't go to the schoolmarm's rescue. His best bet was to wait for daylight and track the guilty party down. Furious at the turn of events, he made his way back to camp.

Amanda and Forbush had not budged. Even so, somehow Mandy's blanket had slipped off her shoulders, so he hiked it to her neck to ward off the growing chill.

Across the road, eyes blazed. The two mongrels were watching him. He collected more firewood and his blanket, then tried to sleep. Worry for Bethany kept him tossing and turning until a faint pink tinge streaked the eastern sky. Rousing himself, he saddled the horses, loaded their supplies onto the pack animal, and was ready to ride out long before sunrise.

The noise Fargo made woke up Mandy. Rubbing her eyes, she said, "What's wrong? Why are we getting ready to move on so early?"

Fargo explained and had her wake Forbush. The lawyer, true to form, complained. "It serves Cole right for coming along. No one asked her to. I was against it from the start, but no one ever listens to me." For some reason he gave Amanda a penetrating look.

Fargo boosted her onto her mount. As he forked leather, he spied wisps of smoke approximately a quarter of a mile to the west. Someone else had camped close to them the night before and he had not even realized it. He was slipping.

"What about breakfast?" Mortimer asked, shuffling to the roan. "It's uncivilized to expect us to rush off like this on an empty stomach."

"You'll live," Fargo said. Kneeing the pinto, he trotted to where Bethany's captor had hidden his horse. The charred brand marked the spot. Since the animal was carrying double, its prints were easy to make out. Fargo pressed on, moving as fast as he dared. About nine in the morning he stopped for a short rest, just long enough to let them quench their thirst at a creek. Mandy was holding up well, but Forbush was as grumpy as a bear just out of hibernation.

"The pain is more than I can stand," Mortimer said. "If we keep going like this, I won't ever be able to sit down again." He rubbed his stomach. "And I'm so hungry, I'm positively nauseated. Can't we at least have some of that wretched jerky you're so fond of?"

Fargo gave each of them a handful. He was under way almost immediately, fearful of having the tracks wiped out by the many riders and wagons using the road. All went well until close to noon. That was when, coming over a hill, he saw two dozen cattle being driven westward by a man and a boy. "Damn!" he snapped.

"What's wrong?" Mandy asked.

"All those cows. They've wiped out the tracks I was following," Fargo said. "From here on out, all we can do is push on and hope for the best."

"Don't fret. We'll find her," Mandy said with the naive confidence typical of one her tender age.

Fargo sincerely hoped so. But as the hours passed and the afternoon waned, his doubts grew. Several times he checked behind them, and twice he thought he saw a solitary rider in the distance, a tall figure in dark clothes. Were they being trailed? Or was it an innocent traveler?

It must have been past four when Fargo rounded a curve and spotted a pair of riders ahead. They were at the side of the road, as if waiting. As he drew closer, he recognized them. One was Jessie, the tough cowboy from the Hotel Excelsior. The other was Weasel, the scruffy frontiersman he had first seen near Darnell's estate in Jefferson City. They stiffened, Jessie placing his right hand on his leg next to his holster. Weasel spat tobacco juice and grinned, exposing teeth so rotten half of them appeared ready to fall out.

"Howdy, mister!" the frontiersman called out amiably. "About time you showed up. We were afraid you had turned around and gone back to Jefferson City."

Fargo reined up in such a fashion that the Ovaro was between the cutthroats and Mandy. She glared at them, while Mortimer shriveled as if attempting the impossible feat of hiding behind his saddle horn.

Weasel winked at Amanda. "Howdy, sweetheart. Ain't seen you in a spell. How have you been?"

Mandy did not answer.

"What's this all about?" Fargo demanded. "What do you want?"

"We want you to come with us," Weasel said. "Our boss needs to see you."

"Tharon Darnell," Fargo stated. "Why is he so interested in Amanda? And how is it that you know her?"

The frontiersman squirted more brown saliva, then wiped his mouth with his stained buckskin sleeve. "Hear that, Jessie. I'm beginnin' to think this feller don't have a clue what's going on."

"Who cares?" the cowboy said. "Our job is to take him to Mr. Darnell, not talk him to death. Let's head out." He wheeled his bay, but when Fargo did not lift a rein, he halted, saying irately, "It wouldn't do to keep Mr. Darnell waiting. He expects us by sundown."

"Give him my regards," Fargo said. "We're not going anywhere with you."

Weasel snickered. "Oh, I reckon you are, mister. Our boss has a powerful temper, you see. It happens that friend of yours is keepin' him company until you show, and if you don't, he might take out his anger on her." Slipping a hand into a pocket, he displayed a long lock of lustrous hair. "This should be familiar."

Fargo's gut balled into a knot. It was Bethany Cole's hair. "That was you last night," he guessed. Only someone with wilderness savvy could have abducted her so handily.

Bending in a mock bow, Weasel said, "The credit is all mine, sure enough. The boss wanted some insurance, as he called it. So he sent me, since I'm the only one in his outfit who can hold a candle to you. It was mighty hard not being caught, I'll admit. You remind me of a jaguar I hunted years back, down on the Mexican border. That critter had eyes in the back of its head, and hardly ever made a mistake."

Jessie gestured. "Enough jawing, old-timer. We have a job to do. Let's get it done."

Weasel sighed and said to Fargo, "Ain't it a shame that the young ones are always so darned impatient? I guess it takes a few gray hairs to teach a man that we all end up six feet under sooner or later. It makes no sense to rush gettin' there." Beckoning Mandy, he said, "Why don't you ride next to me, darlin'? I'd be right pleased to have your company."

"I'd rather drink pigs' blood," Mandy replied.

Wagging a gnarled finger at her, the grizzled frontiersman said, "Is that any way to treat old Weasel? Haven't I always been nice to you? Wasn't it me who snuck you those sweets you like so much whenever I came back from town?"

Mortimer J. Forbush raised a hand like a child in school. "May I speak, gentlemen?"

Jessie's contempt was thick enough to slice with a Green River knife. "What do you want, turncoat?"

"Must I accompany you, too?" the lawyer inquired. "I'd rather not, if that could be arranged."

"It can't," Weasel said flatly. "Mr. Darnell made a special point of tellin' us that we're to drag you back by the scruff of your neck if we have to."

Jessie nodded. "After what you did, you'll be lucky if he doesn't have you skinned alive and staked out over an ant hill."

Mortimer paled. "But I had to go along with her. She made me help."

Both the old-timer and the cowboy laughed, but no warmth mellowed their mirth. It was as hard as granite, as brittle as jagged ice. "Lord, your kind are all alike! You're all as crooked as a rattler in a cactus patch," Weasel declared. "Ain't a one of you can tell the truth, even when your life depends on it."

"But you, Forbush, beat them all!" Jessie said. "You're as dumb as a shovel. Did you honestly think you would get away with it? With all the money Mr. Darnell has? Hell, he'd turn this whole blamed country topsy-turvy looking for her, if that's what it took."

Mortimer fell silent, sagging in despair.

Weasel waved the lock of hair at Fargo. "What's it going to be, big man? Do you come along peaceable-like? Or does Mr. Darnell hurt that pretty lady friend of yours?"

Fury boiled in Fargo, fury he fought down to say, "Lead on." The frontiersman and Jessie headed north, into the woods. Against his better judgment, Fargo did likewise, Mandy at his side. Mortimer brought up the rear, hanging back in fear. "I'd still like to know one thing," he said.

"What would that be?" Weasel responded, glancing over a shoulder.

Fargo nodded at Amanda. "What is Darnell's interest in her?"

Weasel chuckled and said to Jessie, "See? I told you he don't have a clue." Then, facing Fargo, he sobered. "Tharon Darnell is her pappy."

=== 11 ===

In a grassy meadow a mile from the road Tharon Darnell
had pitched camp, and what a camp it was. Five big tents
had been set up for his men. A sixth, even bigger and open
at both ends, was where the cook prepared meals. It also
contained a half-dozen small tables set end to end. A sev-
enth and final tent occupied the center of the meadow, and
this one was the largest and grandest of them all. In fact, it
was the largest tent Skye Fargo had ever laid eyes on.

A string of forty-two horses were picketed to the west,
close to a bubbling creek. To the north, east, and south
grew dense woodland.

Fargo counted fourteen men, the same bunch who had
been with Darnell in Jefferson City, a motley assortment of
rivermen and city ruffians, with a few cowboys sprinkled in
for good measure—men culled from Darnell's many business enterprises; men who would slit the throats of their
own mothers if they were offered enough money.

Most of the cutthroats gathered around an open space in
front of the grand tent as Weasel and Jessie reined up.
Enough rifles were trained on Fargo to turn him into a sieve
if he so much as touched his Colt or Henry. A few of the
men, Fargo noticed, smiled at Mandy, but she ignored
them. Forbush, quaking like an aspen leaf in a thunder-
storm, was mostly ignored.

Weasel went into the grand tent. The glimpse Fargo had
of the interior when the flap parted revealed plush carpet
had been spread on the ground, and fine furnishings added.

Even here, in the midst of the wilderness, Darnell lived in the elegant luxury to which his vast wealth had accustomed him.

The flap parted again. Out came Weasel, to hold it aside so that his employer could emerge.

Tharon Lucien Darnell strode into the sunlight as if he owned the very earth on which he trod. He was a big man, bigger than Fargo, and he wore clothes that would cost most men a year's pay. His hair was so neatly combed and oiled that not a single hair was out of place. Leonine features hinted at latent strength and enormous vitality. He had no weapons that Fargo could see, but then a man like Darnell had no need to carry any. He hired others to be his living weapons.

Looking closely, Fargo saw a remarkable resemblance between Amanda and Darnell. Their foreheads, their cheeks, their chins were all the same. And Darnell, too, had deep blue eyes, only his constantly smoldered like hot coals.

It was to Mandy that Darnell spoke first. Going over to the pony, he laid a hand on her leg and said, "It's good to see you again, precious. I can't tell you how worried I've been."

"I have nothing to say to you, Pa," the girl said stiffly, shifting so he could not touch her. "You had no right to bring us here."

Darnell's smoldering eyes glazed hotter. "I have no right to see my own daughter? That's your mother talking, not you. She's turned you against me, poisoned your mind with her ranting and raving. Well, I won't stand for it. You hear? You're coming with me, and that's final." Seizing her wrist, he yanked her off the pony.

Mandy landed on her feet, but she nearly fell. She swung a tiny fist that had no more effect than would the sting of a bee on a grizzly. "Let go of me!" she said.

Darnell shook her. "Enough! I'm not your mother. I won't tolerate childish behavior."

"Let go!" Mandy insisted, tears welling as she desperately pried at his thick fingers.

Fargo was torn between minding his own business and his affection for Mandy. He had no doubt that Darnell was in truth her father. As such, Darnell had the right to do as he saw fit. But Fargo could not just sit there and let someone who had grown to mean so much to him be manhandled. "You heard the child," he declared. "Take your hand off her."

Tharon Darnell looked up. A fleeting hint of the raw savagery that lurked deep within him was reflected in the feral curl of his lips. Then he composed himself. Adopting a smug, superior air, he released Mandy and turned to the Ovaro. "I'll excuse your bad manners this once. Only because I realize that you are as much a victim in this charade as I am." He gestured at his tent. "Come inside."

Weasel stepped forward. "Do you want us to take his guns, boss?"

"What for?" Darnell said. "From what I've heard, our guest is a reasonable, intelligent man. He's not about to lift a finger against me when he knows that if he does, he will be instantly slain." Darnell paused. "Besides, once he learns how he has been used, I won't be the one he wants to shoot."

"What about him, then?" Weasel asked, nodding at the lawyer.

Darnell seemed to see Forbush for the first time. A shadow darkened his face, and the veins in his temples swelled. "Ah. Mortimer. I can't tell you how it gladdens my heart to see you again."

Forbush looked as if he were about to faint. "Please, Mr. Darnell! Don't be mad at me. She made me, you know. It wasn't my idea."

"Bring them all," Darnell told Weasel and strode into the tent.

Fargo dismounted. He was surprised when Mandy slipped

to his side and stole her hand into his. Squaring his shoulders, he entered.

Tapestries had been hung to divide the tent into compartments. Before them stood a polished mahogany table laden with trays of food and drink. The man called Trevane was slicing cheese and placing it on a plate. He glanced up, regarded Fargo with disdain, and went back to work.

Tharon Darnell had taken a seat facing the opening. His bushy brows knit as he motioned for them to be seated. "Come. You must be famished. Eat hearty. We have much to discuss."

Fargo claimed the right-hand seat so he could keep an eye on the entrance. Mandy moved her chair closer to his, refusing to so much as glance at her father.

Mortimer J. Forbush stepped to the last chair, but did not sit. His legs shaking, he wrung his hands and said, "I know you, Mr. Darnell. I know what you are capable of. What do you plan to do with me?"

"Be seated," Darnell commanded.

When the lawyer hesitated, Trevane put down the cheese and the carving knife, moved around the table, and forcibly steered Forbush into the chair. "Don't make this any harder on yourself than it has to be, Mortimer," the dandy said sternly, then went back to cutting cheese.

Darnell picked up a slice and took a bite. "Delicious," he said. "I import it from Europe. Help yourselves."

"I'm not hungry," Fargo said. To his right a tapestry bulged slightly, as if an elbow had brushed it on the other side. He was the only one who saw it. One of Darnell's gunmen, he suspected, and wondered if there were more.

"Me neither," Mandy said.

"Fair enough," Tharon Darnell stated. "We can eat later." He gave an imperious flick of his fingers. Trevane promptly moved to the tapestry on the left and stood there like a soldier at attention to await his employer's next whim. "I would imagine that you have a few questions you would like answered," Darnell addressed Fargo.

"Just one. What in the hell is going on?"

Darnell gestured toward the rear of the tent. "Miss Cole is back there, alive and well. As for your other question"—he stared at Amanda—"will you tell him, child, or must I?"

Mandy sat as still as a statue. Frowning, he stated, "There was a time, Amanda, when you would listen to me, when we got along the way a father and daughter should."

"That was before I learned what kind of man you are," the girl snapped.

"I hear your mother talking through you," Darnell said. "Yes, I've done some things I shouldn't have. But Rosalie brought them on herself by acting the way she did."

"Ma did nothing wrong," Mandy said.

Fargo saw Darnell's jaw muscles twitch. The man did not take kindly to being talked back to. "I'm still waiting for an explanation," he prodded.

"And you will have one," Darnell said, tearing his gaze from his offspring. Taking a deep breath, he began. "Templeton is my wife's maiden name. We were married twelve years ago this month." His features softened. "She was the loveliest woman I had ever seen, a country girl raised on a farm that bordered property of mine. I was out riding one day and spotted her working in the fields. From that moment, I wanted her. I had to make her mine."

Fargo did not see what any of this had to do with him, but he did not interrupt.

"I wined her and dined her for over a year before she agreed to be my wife," Darnell continued. "We had Amanda, and I was the happiest man alive. But later on things soured. We didn't get along as we once did."

"Tell him why," Mandy said.

Darnell did not reply right away. "Your mother was to blame," he said at last. "She started acting up."

"Ma did no such thing." Mandy turned to Skye. "Pa would hit her all the time and yell at her for no reason. It was awful."

"No reason?" Darnell thundered. "If you were older, you

would understand that I had every right. Your mother was making eyes at every handsome man who came along."

"That's not true!" Mandy said. "You only thought she was being bad!"

Darnell picked up the slice of cheese. But instead of taking a bite, he crushed it and flung it on the carpet. "Enough! I'll be damned if I'll sit here and take such talk from you, even if you are my own flesh and blood."

To divert Darnell's wrath from Mandy, Fargo said, "You must have taken it hard when your wife died."

Darnell was slow to simmer down. Scowling, he said, "She's as alive as you and I. Her death was a sham, a ruse to get me killed."

"How's that?" Fargo said.

Stabbing a finger at the lawyer, Darnell said, "I'll let Mortimer explain. After all, my dearly beloved could not have carried out her wicked little scheme without his invaluable help. Isn't that so, Mortimer?"

Forbush gripped the arms of his chair and licked his thin lips. "What else could I do? You know how persuasive your wife can be."

"Bull," Darnell said. "You did it for the money. I know about the ten thousand dollars she paid you, the five thousand she paid that hick doctor to have a fake death certificate made, and the two thousand she gave Winslow, the undertaker, to have him bury an empty coffin."

Forbush groaned.

Darnell turned to Fargo. "I was in England at the time. I had been there for four months when I received a letter from a doctor I had never heard of telling me that my wife had come down with consumption shortly after I left, and claiming she wasn't long for this world. I took the first ship out of London, but when I reached St. Louis, Rosalie was supposedly dead and buried."

"How do I figure into this?" Fargo asked. "I doubt I've ever met your wife."

"You'd remember her if you did," Darnell said. "No one ever forgets that golden hair of hers."

"She's a blonde?" Fargo said, jolted. He remembered the mystery woman in the cloak he had chased through Jefferson City, the one as fleet as an antelope who had slipped through his fingers in the field. A blonde woman. No wonder she had been so fast, so crafty. She was a country girl, born and bred. "Forbush told me that she had auburn hair."

"Another of his many lies," Darnell sneered. "As for where you fit in, he can tell you better than I can."

Fargo glanced at the lawyer, who squirmed like a worm on a hook. "The truth," he directed. "All of it."

Mortimer's throat bobbed. "It was her idea! I swear it! She thought that by setting you up as Mandy's father, it would put Tharon and you at each other's throats."

"In other words," Darnell said dryly, "she knew that I would stop at nothing to get my daughter back, and she was hoping you would kill me to stop me."

It was unbelievable, Fargo reflected. He had been used, like a pawn in a chess game. Searing resentment coursed through him. "But why *me*?" he rasped. "Why did she pick a total stranger?"

"Rosalie got the idea from the newspapers," Mortimer said. "She'd read a lot of stories about you. About your reputation as a ladies' man. About all the Indians you've fought and all the men you've killed. You were the one man she felt could stand up to Tharon and win."

Fargo shook his head, flabbergasted. His own notoriety was to blame! Who would have thought it? Simply being who he was had nearly gotten him killed. "I'll be damned," he said, then grew aware that Forbush was still talking.

"—worked it out almost a full year ago. But she had to wait for Tharon to leave on one of his extended business trips before she could put it into effect. My original orders were to travel to Denver and points west to find you. It was sheer dumb luck that you stumbled on us when you did."

"Luck?" Fargo said, feeling an urge to hit someone. Anyone. "There were men out to *kill* me."

Darnell spoke. "Not any of mine. I told my boys to find out where Mandy was and bring her back. They were to rough you up some if need be, but that was all."

"Did Clem and Hiram work for you?" Fargo inquired.

"Never heard of them."

Both Fargo and Darnell swung toward Forbush, who started to rise. At a gesture from Darnell, Trevane darted over, clamped a hand on the lawyer's shoulder, and pushed him back down. "You'll stay put, scum, until Mr. Darnell says otherwise."

Mortimer glanced wildly around, like a terrified animal that wanted to bolt. "I have nothing else to say," he whined.

"Oh, I think you do," Darnell said and nodded at Trevane, who suddenly grasped Forbush's wrist and twisted sharply, provoking a yelp. "Talk, or I'll have him break your arm."

"All right!" Mortimer cried, struggling in vain to free himself. Bent sideways, he blurted, "I was the one who hired Clem and Hiram. I was afraid that if Fargo nosed around in St. Louis, he might learn the truth sooner or later. So I paid them to break a few bones to keep him from leaving Jefferson City."

"Did Rosalie go along with the idea?" Fargo asked, recalling the meeting between the blonde and the lawyer at the Imperial.

"No. She ordered me to call them off. But by then it was too late. They had already jumped you."

Tharon Darnell leaned toward Forbush. "Where is my wife right this minute, you stinking son of a bitch?"

"I'm right behind you, Tharon."

Everyone whirled.

Through a gap in the tapestries had stepped Rosalie Darnell, a gold-plated Colt clutched in her right hand. She had on a long burgundy dress and the same cloak she had worn in Jefferson City. Pointing the Colt at her husband, she thumbed back the hammer. "Not a peep out of you, Tharon. Try to call your men, and so help me, I'll kill you where you sit."

Darnell made no sudden moves. When Trevane started to sidle to the left, he shook his head.

"Ma!" Mandy happily exclaimed, rushing around the table to throw her arms around her mother's legs. "I knew you wouldn't be far away! Just like you promised!"

Rosalie stooped to lovingly cradle her daughter in her free arm. "A person should always keep their word," she said tenderly.

"You're a fine one to talk," Tharon scoffed.

Paying no attention to her husband, Rosalie, appearing nervous, studied Fargo. "I'm truly sorry for all the misery I put you through. I know it was horribly wrong. But I was desperate. I needed out of my marriage, and I knew that the only way I could get out was if Tharon was dead."

"So you set me up to pull the trigger for you," Fargo said accusingly.

"If it hadn't been you, it would have been someone else. You were just convenient." Rosalie straightened and edged toward the gap in the tapestries. "I wish I could make you understand, Mr. Fargo. I wish you could have seen him beat me, day in and day out. If I so much as looked at another man, he'd fly into a rage. It got so bad, I couldn't even say hello to the clerk at the general store."

Tharon Darnell glowered.

"So long as he only hurt me, I could handle it," Rosalie said. "But then he began to slap Mandy around, too. That was the last straw."

Darnell shrugged. "You make me sound like some sort of ogre. A man has the right to keep his children in line."

Rosalie shook her head while continuing to move toward the gap. "To discipline them, yes, but not by hitting them so hard that they're left black and blue. Not by smacking them across the face. Or by taking a switch to a girl Mandy's age."

"She broke a rare vase—" Darnell tried to counter.

"It was an *accident*," Rosalie said, her voice trembling with pent-up emotion. "She bumped into the table it was on by mistake. You had no cause to hit her as many times as you did." She paused. "If I hadn't stopped you when I did, I honestly think you would have beaten her until she bled. Just as you've done to me on occasion."

Fargo made no attempt to hide the disgust he felt for Tharon Darnell. His resentment toward Rosalie was dwindling with each new revelation. He was beginning to see why she had done what she did. It had been the frantic act of a woman at the end of her tether, of someone with no one to turn to, someone with no other hope for herself or her little girl.

"So what now, beloved?" asked Darnell with thinly veiled sarcasm. "Do you expect me to let you waltz out of here with Amanda, just like that?" He snapped his fingers.

"Try to stop us, and people will die," Rosalie pledged. "We have our own lives to live, and we want to live them as far from you as possible."

"What about Fargo?" Darnell said. "He would be in his legal right to press charges against you. Frankly, I hope he does. I'll gladly testify on his behalf. It would serve you right to spend a few years behind bars."

All eyes swung toward the Trailsman. Fargo never hesitated. "I won't be pressing charges," he said, and rose. "As a matter of fact, I side with your wife, Darnell. You're a bastard, plain and simple."

The change that came over Tharon Darnell was startling. His face contorted into a mask of hatred so vicious, so ugly, that he resembled a rabid beast more than he did a sane human being. The true nature of his wicked soul was exposed, the vile, debased character of a man who regarded his word as the supreme law and who would punish anyone who transgressed against him. "No one talks to me like that," he snarled.

Fargo moved around the table, careful not to take his

gaze off Darnell. "If you'll let me," he told the wife, "I'd be honored to help you get away from here."

"You would?" Rosalie said, hope sparkling in her lovely eyes. "After what I've done? After all the trouble I've caused you?"

"Let's just say that this girl of yours can grow on a man," Fargo said, smiling at Mandy, who glanced beyond him and opened her mouth to shout. Almost too late he realized that Trevane was gliding toward him. Trevane's manicured hand had already dived into his long coat. Pivoting, Fargo palmed his Colt, bringing the dandy to a halt, a fancy dagger half drawn. "That's close enough."

Trevane glanced at Darnell, who indicated he should drop the dagger. He did so, scowling. "My time will come, Trailsman. Wait and see."

"Goodbye, Tharon," Rosalie said. "Please have the decency to let us live in peace. Think of us as a closed chapter in your life, and everything will be fine."

Darnell practically crackled with tension. "You walk out on me!" he spat. "You steal our daughter. You try to have me killed. And you have the gall to demand that I act like nothing has happened?" His hands closed and twisted, as if he were wrenching her neck. "Woman, mark my words. You will suffer for this outrage. If it takes every penny I have, if it takes the rest of my life, I will hunt you down and make you atone for your sins."

"Please, Tharon. I'm begging you. For old time's sake," Rosalie pleaded.

"My only regret," Darnell intoned, "is that I didn't hit you hard enough to beat some sense into that stupid head of yours. You, and the brat's."

"Pa!" Mandy cried.

Sadness crept over Rosalie, sadness so deep, so intense, that it would have touched a heart of stone. Yet it had no effect on her husband. She went to say more, but at that juncture the front flap swung open and in rushed Carver,

139

the gunman from Texas, one of the four who had jumped Fargo in Jefferson City.

"Boss! Boss! Come quick! We're surrounded by a passel of hombres with rifles! And they don't look none too friendly." Accenting the Texan's point was the crack of a shot. Voices were raised in anger. "I think they're marauders, Mr. Darnell," Carver said. "And it looks to me as if they're out for our blood."

ie gunman from Texas, one of the four who had jumped
Fargo in Jefferson City.

Wash Rose frantically gestured. Gesturing and
n hoarse, excruciating whisper, "Gets out. Went
surely we wouldn't win, we'd lost," word.

$$=========12=========$$

In his excited state, the Texan had not noticed at first that
Skye Fargo held a pistol trained on Tharon Darnell. Now
Carver did, and stepping back, he poised his hand to draw,
saying, "What's goin' on here? Want me to plug this varmint,
Mr. Darnell?"

"Don't be a fool," Darnell declared. "You're not that fast."

"Want to bet?" Carver said, and true to the impulsive
trademark of his wild and reckless breed, he went for his
six-gun.

Fargo shot him in the shoulder. The slug jolted the gunman sideways, his revolver sliding from fingers suddenly
gone limp. Staggering, he pressed a hand to the spurting
wound. Fargo swung toward the entrance, expecting more
killers to rush to Darnell's aid, but a flurry of gunfire had
erupted at the moment he squeezed the trigger. Apparently
no one outside had noticed the single shot in the grand tent.
"On your feet," he directed Darnell. "Lead the way."

Trevane stepped away from the table as Fargo ushered
Darnell to the opening, the muzzle of his pistol gouging
Darnell's spine. One of the millionaire's underlings lay in a
spreading pool of blood a few dozen yards off. The rest
were ringed around the open space between the tents, all
eyes on the tree line. In the trees furtive figures moved. A
glance confirmed that the marauders had the meadow surrounded.

The firing had ceased. Darnell moved into the open,

Fargo glued to his back. Jessie and Weasel saw them and came running.

"There must be thirty of 'em, I reckon," the frontiersman reported. "They haven't let us know what they want yet, but it's pretty clear they're up to no good." Weasel indicated the dead man. "They shot Haslett, there, for no damn reason at all."

"What do we do, boss?" Jessie asked. "The boys and me will rush the polecats if you give the word."

A riverman crouched beside the cook tent called out, "Look! Here comes one on a horse! Do we shoot him?"

The rider held a long thin branch, at the end of which a dirty white handkerchief had been tied. Waving it, grinning arrogantly, he brazenly crossed toward the grand tent.

"No firing!" Darnell yelled. "We'll hear him out." He glanced at Fargo and said so only they could hear, "We both know what's going to happen. And we both know I can't do what has to be done with you trodding on my wheels. I propose a truce until this is over. You have my word that neither I nor any of my men will lay a finger on you or my wife or Amanda. Agreed?"

Fargo nodded curtly. He had no other option. He could not hold Darnell at gunpoint and protect Rosalie and Mandy at the same time.

The man on the horse passed between two of the smaller tents, then drew rein. He was a rat in human guise, his clothes shabby and filthy, his face streaked with grime, his whiskers straggly and splotched with dirt and tobacco stains. Wedged under his belt were three pistols. The hilt of a butcher knife jutted from his left boot. Beady eyes swept the encampment, then settled on Darnell. "You must be top dog here. So I'll tell you how it is."

"I'm listening," Darnell said.

Resting the truce flag across his saddle, the rider said, "My name is Collindar. Me and those coons in the woods have formed us a militia to help the South in the coming war between the states. Whatever we need, we take. It's as simple as that."

Darnell scanned the edge of the meadow. "You think so, do you?"

"Mister, I *know* so," Collindar snapped. "We've got us thirty guns to your dozen or so. Buck us, and you'll go out in a smear of gore. Do as we say, and you get to live."

"What is it that you want?" Darnell asked.

Collindar bobbed his chin toward the string. "All of your horses. All of your guns. All of your money. And most of your grub."

"Is that all?" Tharon Darnell said, his tone flinty. "Why don't you take the tents and our clothes, as well?

"Hell, we're not greedy," Collindar said. "That's why we'll let you keep enough food to see your through until you reach a town."

"You're all heart," Darnell said, casually stepping closer to the horse. "What about my wife and young daughter? Will you grant them safe passage?"

Collindar smirked. "There's a woman here? We didn't know that. Some of the boys ain't seen a female in weeks."

Darnell took another casual step. "Do you have any idea who I am?"

"I don't rightly care," Collindar said. "Just some idiot who didn't know enough not to traipse off into the wilds when the whole countryside is up in arms." He chortled. "We're right glad you came along when you did, mister. Our mounts are plumb tuckered out, and we're low on food."

"That's too bad," Darnell said, "because you're not getting a single morsel from us." Drawing himself up to his full height, he stated, "I'm Tharon Lucien Darnell. Perhaps you've heard of me. If so, you'll tuck your tail between your legs like the cur you are and ride off before I give the order for my men to open fire."

Collindar looked mad enough to spit nails. Flushing, he spat, "Your name don't mean diddly to me. And if it's a fight you want, it's a fight you'll get." He began to raise his reins.

"Do you honestly think I'll let you leave?"

The marauder froze. "Now you hold on! I came in here under a white flag. That means I get to ride out again, safe and sound."

"Says who?" Darnell taunted him. "You're not part of a duly constituted militia. You have no legal right to confiscate my property. All you are is a bandit, trying to rob us. And that means I have every right to break your scrawny neck if I want. Which is just what I'm going to do." So saying, Darnell lunged, grabbed Collindar by the arm and leg, and heaved the marauder to the ground. "Kill them!" he bellowed. "Kill every last one!"

Bedlam ensued. Darnell's men cut loose, unleashing a hailstorm of lead that caught the bandits by surprised. But the marauders were quick to recover and to return fire. Within seconds slugs were flying thick and furious. Men screamed, cursed, shouted.

Fargo ducked low as slugs peppered the ground around him, and the air above him buzzed to the passage of leaded hornets. He saw Darnell, heedless of the swarm, pin Collindar with a knee and clamp his hands around Collindar's neck.

Swiveling, Fargo dashed toward the grand tent. A handful of renegades had rushed the camp and were battling Darnell's men near the cook tent. As he went by, one of the marauders burst through and pumped a rifle to his shoulder. Fargo fired twice, dropping the bandit in his tracks. Then he plunged through the opening.

Mortimer J. Forbush was still in his chair, hunched over with his hands over his ears. Tears stained his cheeks.

Mandy was on her side on the carpet, blood trickling from the corner of her mouth.

Over in a corner, Rosalie fought Trevane. The dandy was striving to pin her arms to her sides, and she was resisting with all her might. Neither noticed Fargo rush toward them. He brought the barrel of his Colt crashing down on Trevane's head, and as the dandy crumpled, shoved him aside. "Are you all right?"

"Fine," Rosalie said breathlessly. "But Mandy! He hit her!"

Together, they darted to the girl, both kneeling to gently ease the child onto her back. Mandy's eyes opened, and she tried to sit up, but her mother would not let her. "How do you feel? Are you dizzy? Can you see?"

"I'm fine, Ma," Mandy said.

The heavy boom of rifles mixed with the lighter crack of pistols had risen to a thunderous crescendo. As Fargo raised his head to listen, several stray shots ripped through the tent, one thudding into the table. "We have to get out of here," he said. Even as he spoke, a shadowy shape filled the front opening. Into the tent hurtled a marauder as grimy and scruffy as Collindar. Ablaze with blood lust, he spotted Forbush and brought his rifle up. Mortimer, paralyzed with fright, just sat there.

Fargo was a shade faster. His Colt banged, punching the renegade backward, out the entrance. There was not a moment to lose. Gripping Mandy's arm, he hauled her erect. "We have to find the schoolmarm, then get out of here."

Rosalie, nodding, guided her daughter toward the tapestries. "I cut a hole in the rear when Tharon and his men were all out front. We can get out that way."

Fargo slowed and beckoned to the lawyer. "What are you waiting for? No matter who wins, you're a dead man. Come on with us."

"You'd let me?" Mortimer said in amazement, springing after them. "After what I did?"

Turning, Fargo ran to catch up with Rosalie and Amanda. He still disliked the man, but he had to give Forbush credit for helping the mother and daughter when they needed help most. For a craven coward like Mortimer to go up against a man of Darnell's stature had taken a lot of gumption. Fargo's estimation of Forbush had risen several notches.

The tapestries had been hung in such a manner that narrow aisles wound through them. Down these Rosalie raced, winding deeper and deeper into the enormous tent.

Fargo passed an opening into another spacious section and drew up short. "Hold up!" he shouted. Dashing in, he squatted beside Bethany Cole, who had been bound hand and foot, and gagged. It only took half a minute to free her.

"What's happening?" the schoolmarm asked in alarm.

"No time to explain. Just stick close and keep your head down," Fargo advised, helping her stand.

They ran down another aisle, then took a left. "Here it is!" Rosalie exclaimed, parting a five-foot rent.

"Let me go first," Fargo cautioned, shouldering past her. Poking his head out, he squinted against the glare. Another tent was forty feet away. Between the two lay a dead marauder, the top of his head blown clean off. No others were in sight, although the battle raged fiercely all around.

"We have to reach the trees," Fargo said, covering the others as they emerged. "Stay close to me." Bending, he zigzagged. Off to the right a man screeched. Off to the left a shotgun went off.

No shots were directed at them. Fargo reached the side of the smaller tent and hunkered. In the forest figures moved, bandits swinging around the camp to the west to help their companions.

Mortimer J. Forbush was a nervous wreck. Every shot made him flinch. Every scream made him paler. "What are we waiting for?" he anxiously demanded. "The coast is clear." Leaping to his feet, he sped toward the trees.

"Mortimer, don't!" Bethany cried.

Forbush had barely covered ten feet when he was spun half around by a slug that ripped through his back at an angle and exploded out of his chest. Stunned, he tottered, feebly covering the exit wound in a vain bid to stanch the scarlet river flowing from it. He looked toward Rosalie, his mouth working.

"Dear God!" Rosalie cried. "We have to help him!" She started to rise, but Fargo snagged her arm.

"Run out there and you'll get the same thing he did. Is that what you want?"

"We can't just—" Rosalie said, gasping when Mortimer was struck a second time, in the stomach. The impact bowled him over. She struggled to go to him, saying, "Please! He might still be alive!"

Forbush was. Weakly, he raised his head, his eyes vacant, his mouth agape. Drooling crimson drops, he rose onto his hands and knees. His left hand extended toward them in eloquent appeal. The next shot caught him full in the forehead.

"No! No! No!" Rosalie wailed, slumping against Fargo. "He was the only true friend I had. The only one willing to stand up to Tharon."

Mandy was crying. Fargo shoved her into her mother's arms. "We'll wind up just like him unless you do exactly as I say. Savvy?" Without waiting for an answer, he moved to the corner. Taking a peek, he saw marauders and some of Darnell's men swapping shots and blows to the south. Darnell's cutthroats were holding their own. So far.

"Take my hand," Fargo directed Rosalie. She complied, then took Mandy's, and Mandy grasped Bethany's. "Ready?"

All three of them nodded.

Hurling himself into the open, Fargo ran. He had to go much slower than he would have liked in order for Mandy to keep up. It was nerve-wracking, being so exposed, so vulnerable. The skin between his shoulder blades prickled. His scalp itched. They had gone a few steps beyond the lawyer's body when a slug whizzed past.

Fargo spun. A marauder with a rifle stood beside the next tent to the south. It had to be the same man who had dropped Mortimer. Extending his Colt, Fargo fired at the same split second the rifleman did. An invisible finger tugged at his hat. The marauder threw up his arms, reeled, tripped over a stake, and toppled.

Fargo jogged on, alert for threats. Fortunately, the majority of the marauders were too busy fighting Darnell's men to try and stop them. He was glad when they crashed into the sheltering brush. Squatting, he surveyed the meadow, seeking the Ovaro.

The pinto and their other mounts had been added to the string west of camp. In the violent melee the animals had been largely forgotten. Many were in a panic, nickering and stomping and tossing their heads.

"We have to reach those horses," Fargo said. On foot, they would be easy pickings. On horseback, they had a fair chance of escaping alive. He threaded among the trees, skirting the meadow.

The marauders had penetrated the camp on the north and south, but were being held back by fierce resistance. Both sides hid behind tents and tables, swapping shots at random. Bodies littered the grass. Somewhere, Tharon Darnell roared encouragement to his men.

Fargo stepped over a log and was nearing a thicket when a metallic rasp overhead drew his attention to a bandit perched in the fork of a tree. The man was taking precise aim with a Sharps at one of Darnell's men.

"Hey!" Fargo called out. The marauder glanced down, swore, and twisted to point his rifle at them. Fargo flicked his thumb. His Colt spewed lead and smoke.

The man high above was kicked from his roost. Grasping his throat, the marauder plunged. He screamed, his death cry chopped off by the thud of his body hitting the earth. His rifle clattered from limb to limb and fell into the thicket.

Fargo did not stop to verify the man was dead. They were losing too much precious time as it was. Eventually, one side or the other would come out on top, and he did not want to be there when that happened.

Occasional slugs tore through the growth. Trunks were smacked, limbs sheared, leafs shredded. The firing soon tapered. Not because either faction had won. No, they were picking their targets with more care to conserve their ammunition.

"Owww!" Mandy suddenly howled, clutching her shin.

Fearing she had been shot, Fargo hovered over Rosalie and Bethany while the pair inspected the child's leg. A ragged gash marked where Mandy had scraped it against the jagged end of a fallen limb. Otherwise, she was fine.

"We can't linger," Fargo pointed out.

"I know," Rosalie said, sliding her arms under her daughter and lifting. "Don't slow down on our account. We'll keep up. I promise."

"I'm fine, Ma," Mandy protested, wriggling. "Put me down. I can walk on my own."

"Hush, child," Rosalie scolded. "I won't chance losing you. I could never stand to go on living if that were to happen." She pecked Mandy on the forehead. "You're all I have in this world, precious."

Fargo went on. The firing had died to a trickle. It was a stalemate, but that would not last long—knowing Tharon Darnell. Movement among the tents on the west edge of the camp hinted that Darnell was attempting to outflank his enemies. The wounded Carver and Weasel were among those Fargo spotted.

The horses had quieted some. Fargo came to the tree which anchored one end of the rope. A sorrel nickered as he crept toward the middle of the string, where the Ovaro, Mandy's pony, and their pack animals were tied.

"Look!" Rosalie whispered.

A marauder was crawling toward the horses from the north. Clamped between his teeth was a big knife. Clearly, he intended to cut the horses loose and run them off while his companions kept Darnell's outfit busy.

Fargo couldn't let that happen. "Stay here," he whispered, holstering his Colt. Drawing the Arkansas toothpick, he ducked under the rope and stalked forward.

The burly marauder was worried about being shot in the back. Again and again he paused to glance out over the meadow. He did not devote much attention to the string, enabling Fargo to reach the second to the last horse without being seen. Coiling, he peered under the legs of the last animal.

The marauder had risen into a crouch. Taking the knife from his mouth, he moved toward the tree the rope was looped around.

Fargo inched nearer, elbow bent, the toothpick held close to his chest. A single thrust should suffice. He came abreast of the last horse, a bay, which stared at him a moment, then whinnied at the top of its lungs.

The marauder whirled around. A curse heralded his attack as he threw himself at Fargo with his long blade flashing. Fargo, retreating, was hard pressed to counter the blows. The ring of steel on steel pealed across the meadow. A feint by the outlaw forced Fargo to back into the horses. A dun shoved him with its nose, propelling him at his adversary. He dodged a stroke that would have cleaved his midriff open, then parried a thrust to the jugular.

Circling, the marauder tried a low slash, then a high. His skill spoke for itself. Fargo barely evaded the last one. Skipping aside, he bumped into the rope and would have gone over if the marauder had not pounced and missed. It gave Fargo something to grab—the man's shirt.

Pulling upward, Fargo sheared the toothpick between the marauder's ribs, to the hilt. Something warm and sticky gushed over his fingers. He twisted the knife, driving it deeper, and the man grunted and gurgled and became as limp as an empty sack. Fargo shoved the man from him, then was startled to have Mandy briskly hobble into his arms.

"Thank goodness! I thought he was going to kill you!"

Rosalie and Bethany were with her, Rosalie holding the gold-plated Colt. She squeezed his shoulder, saying, "I'm sorry. We couldn't stay there and do nothing while you risked your life on our behalf. It wouldn't have been right."

Fargo was deeply touched. Most men would give their eyeteeth to have a wife like Rosalie and a daughter like Amanda, yet Tharon Lucien Darnell treated them as if they were his personal whipping posts, never taking how they felt into account. The man was so blinded by wealth and power that he never realized his true treasures were his own family.

"We must hurry," Fargo said. Other marauders might get the same idea the dead one had. Shooing Mandy and the women before him, he came to the center of the string. First he cut Mandy's pony free, then a dun for Rosalie, a sorrel for Bethany, and the Ovaro. "Mount up," he said, stepping to the packhorse.

A volley from the woods to the north snapped Fargo's head up. Five marauders were charging them.

"Skye!" Mandy shrieked.

"Ride!" Fargo shouted. Gripping the saddle horn, he swung onto his saddle and slapped his legs against the pinto's sides. The stallion exploded out of there as if its tail were on fire. Yanking the Henry from the scabbard, he blazed away. It had the desired effect of scattering the renegades. In moments the schoolmarm and the other two reached the trees to the south. He fired a final shot, then joined them.

"Will they come after us?" Rosalie wondered.

It looked that way. The five dashed to the string and were preparing to mount when a staccato exchange of gunfire broke out in the vicinity of the tents. Forgetting all else, they ran off to assist their band.

Fargo trotted southward, eager to reach the road before nightfall. It would take some hard riding. Already the sun had partially dipped below the western rim of the world, and the shadows were lengthening.

It did not bother Fargo that they had no water and little food. He had been living off the land for so long, it was second nature. And he had enough jerky and pemmican in his saddlebags to last a couple of days if they rationed it.

Rosalie brought the dun up next to the pinto. "I can't thank you enough for what you've done."

"Save your thanks for when you're safe," Fargo said. He

didn't mention that so long as Darnell was alive, she would never know a moment's peace. The poor woman would spend the rest of her life looking over her shoulder, never knowing when her husband's heavy hand might fall on it.

As if she could read his thoughts, Rosalie commented, "Maybe the renegades will kill him. Maybe Mandy and I can get on with our lives at long last."

Fargo did not say so, but he was confident it would take more than a motley band of marauders to put an end to Tharon Lucien Darnell. And once Darnell either drove them off or exterminated them to the last man, he would come after his wife and daughter.

Fargo rode faster.

Close to midnight, Skye Fargo finally called a halt. He wanted to push on through the night, but Mandy was not up to it. She could not keep her eyes open. When Rosalie cried out and grabbed her dozing daughter to keep Mandy from falling, he reluctantly veered into the trees. At the first open space he reined up.

Rosalie lifted Mandy off the pony, spread out the girl's blankets, and tucked her in. Mandy mumbled a few words and was immediately sound asleep.

Wearily rising, Rosalie ran a hand through her long flaxen hair. "We should be safe enough here," she said. "Even if they guess which way we went, they can't track us in the dark."

Fargo was not so sure. Weasel might be able to. It all depended on what Tharon Darnell had done when he reached the road. Had he gone on toward St. Louis, assuming they had done the same? Or had he headed west toward Jefferson City, as they were doing? If the former, they were safe.

Then another, more disturbing, possibility occurred to him. What if Darnell had split up his men, sending half east and half west? It was what Fargo would have done if he were in Darnell's boots. "You two can turn in," he instructed Rosalie and the schoolmarm. "I'll keep watch."

"It's not fair to put the burden on your shoulders. We should take turns," Bethany proposed. "Why don't you rest first? I'll wake you in a few hours."

"I'm fine," Fargo said, although fatigue had been nipping

at him for the past couple of hours. "You ladies need to sleep more than I do."

Rosalie, to his surprise, came over and gently placed a hand on his cheek. "To think, what I did to you! I'm so sorry. I should have found another way."

"It's forgotten already," Fargo lied, for as long as he lived he would never forget this magnificent woman and her exceptional daughter. While she and Bethany Cole turned in, he tended to the horses. Then, cradling the Henry, he walked to a stump on the south edge of the clearing and took a seat.

The night was quiet. No coyotes were abroad. No breeze blew. A few crickets and the like chirped on occasion, that was all. Fargo leaned the Henry against the stump and folded his arms. He was more tired than he had thought, and soon his eyelids grew heavy. Shaking himself, he straightened. But soon he had to do it again. And again.

With a start, Fargo snapped his eyes open and sat up for what had to be the tenth or eleventh time. Right away he sensed that something was wrong, dreadfully wrong. He had slept without meaning to. The position of the stars told him that it was close to four. And off in the woods, something was moving.

Fargo started to rise. Cold metal brushed the back of the neck, and a colder voice whispered, "Sit still, mister. One twitch and my trigger finger is liable to jerk."

It was Weasel. Other figures loomed out of the darkness. Two, three, four of them. They quietly spread out, ringing the mother and daughter. Except for one, who planted his feet in front of Fargo. "We meet again, bastard," Tharon Darnell hissed.

Fargo never saw the blow that caught him on the jaw. He landed on his back behind the stump and made a grab for his Colt. The muzzle of Weasel's Sharps, jammed against his cheek, froze him in place.

"Don't try it, you ornery polecat."

With the frontiersman and Darnell were Carver, Jessie,

and Trevane. The dandy snatched Fargo's revolver and jammed it under his own belt, then hauled Fargo erect and pushed him toward their employer.

Tharon Darnell gripped Fargo's shirt and drew back a fist. "I'm going to enjoy this, Trailsman. First I'll bust you up, bone by bone, then I'll stomp you into the dirt and leave you for the buzzards." He glanced at the sleeping forms of the women and Amanda, and suddenly pushed Fargo aside. "But my loving family should be awake. It's only right that they see what happens to anyone who opposes me."

"Not the girl, too," Fargo said. Hardly were the words out of his mouth than Darnell whipped around and planted a fist in the pit of his stomach. Pain lanced through him, and he doubled over, a bitter taste in his mouth.

"When I want your opinion, I'll ask for it," Tharon Darnell growled.

Bethany Cole sat up. She opened her mouth, probably to warn Rosalie and Mandy, but Jessie grabbed her from behind and rammed his pistol against her cheek. That shut her up.

Rosalie stirred. Darnell nudged her with a toe and she rolled onto her back, opening her eyes. His leering face was the first thing she saw. Panic brought her up off the ground, the gold-plated Colt materializing as if by magic in her right hand. She got off a shot, but Tharon had seized her wrist and the slug plowed harmlessly into the earth.

"Is this any way to greet your doting husband?" Darnell mocked her, wrenching the Colt from her grasp. Tossing it down, he backhanded Rosalie across the face, rocking her on her heels. "That's just for starters. Before I'm done, you'll rue the day you ever tried to leave me." He gripped her throat.

No one but Fargo had noticed that Mandy had sat up and was glaring at her father. Bending, she picked up the Colt with both hands, pointed it at him, and awkwardly thumbed back the hammer. The distinct click riveted everyone where they stood.

"Amanda!" Tharon Darnell said. "Put that down! Now!"

"Let go of Ma," Mandy said, her expression grim. "Do it, Pa, or so help me, I'll shoot you."

Carver, who was behind the girl, edged forward and trained his pistol on her, but Darnell stopped him with a furious oath, adding, "Stand still, you jackass! No harm must come to her, no matter what!"

Mandy slid out from under the blankets and stepped back so she could see all of them. "I won't tell you again, Pa," she warned. "Take your hand off of Ma."

"Sure, sugar. Whatever you say." Smiling broadly, Darnell relaxed his grip and lowered his arm. "There. See. Now put down that gun."

"No," Mandy said.

Darnell's temper almost got the better of him. Clenching his fists, he took a step, stopping when she jerked the pistol higher, aiming it at his face.

"Don't!" Rosalie shouted and leaped to prevent her daughter from firing. In her anxiety and haste she blundered between Tharon and Mandy, and Tharon was quick to take advantage of the mistake. He shoved Rosalie hard, pushing her against Amanda. Mother and daughter tumbled down in a tangle of limbs, the revolver going off with a muffled retort.

Fargo rose as they fell, surging to his feet with the toothpick in his right hand. Trevane, who was watching the Darnells, spun and brought up his cane to deflect the thrust. The toothpick glanced off the cane, sliced across Trevane's arm, and sheared into the dandy's side. As Trevane threw himself backward, Fargo grabbed his Colt, and whirled.

Carver and Jessie were swinging toward him. The Texan was the quickest, his pistol cracking at the same instant Fargo's did. Carver's shot missed Fargo's head by the width of a hair, but Fargo's slug hit home. Carver staggered as Fargo shifted and banged a shot at Jessie.

Simultaneously, other guns had boomed. Darnell bellowed, "Don't shoot her! Don't shoot her!" Someone swore luridly. Feet drummed, and underbrush crackled.

Sudden silence fell. Fargo spun. Rosalie was on her knees, holding her smoking Colt. Bethany had an arm around Mandy. Darnell, Trevane, and Weasel were nowhere to be seen.

Fargo crouched and turned back. Jessie was prone and lifeless, but Carver was still on his feet, swaying, struggling to raise his six-gun. "Drop it," Fargo said.

Carver grit his teeth and spat, "Go to hell!" His Colt was almost level.

"After you," Fargo said, and shot the Texan smack between the eyes. As Carver crumpled, he dashed over to Rosalie, who was pale and had an inky stain on the side of her dress. "You've been shot."

"When we fell, my gun went off," she answered. Gamely, she attempted to rise. "I tried to shoot Tharon and the others, but they ran."

"Weasel was going to shoot her. Pa wouldn't let him," Mandy mentioned.

"Only because Tharon wants to punish me," Rosalie said. "He can't beat me black and blue if I'm dead."

Replacing his knife, Fargo helped her to stand. Warm blood coated his palm. Her wound needed to be examined, but they could not stay there in the open. "We have to get you under cover." With her leaning against his shoulder, and Bethany safeguarding Mandy, they hurried into the trees. Beside an oak, Fargo stopped and eased her down.

"Where do you think Pa and those other men got to?" Mandy whispered.

Fargo was wondering the same thing. They would not go far. Tharon would not let his wife and daughter get away again.

There was no telling what Darnell would do with Bethany Cole, but Fargo's own fate was not hard to predict. Darnell would have him picked off. So long as he stayed near Rosalie and Mandy, it was doubtful Darnell's cutthroats would shoot. But he had never been one to hide behind a woman's skirts. "Don't move from this spot," he whispered. "One way or the other, this ends here and now."

Rosalie clutched him. "It's not your fight. It's mine. You can still reach your horse and ride off. Take Mandy with you."

"I'm not leaving you, Ma," the child said.

"That makes two of us," Fargo whispered and slipped off into the night before Rosalie could object. He looped toward the clearing, going from trunk to trunk. West of him a twig snapped. A vague shape flittered through high weeds. He took a hasty bead, but the shape vanished.

Fargo stalked the stalker. It had to be Darnell or Trevane. Weasel would never make that much noise. Bent at the knees, he entered the weeds, careful not to rustle them. To the northwest something swished, so he slanted in that direction.

Abruptly, the wilderness was rocked by the boom of a heavy-caliber rifle. It was Weasel's Sharps. The slug drilled into the earth under him. Fargo flung himself flat and rolled to the right. The shot had come from the southwest, from a stand of pines.

A seasoned frontiersman could reload a Sharps in five to ten seconds. Fargo had that long to get out of there. Scrambling onto his hands and knees, he hurtled into the trees. Behind a maple, he halted.

Fargo slowly straightened. He probed the pines, but they were mired in blackest shadow. Weasel had picked an ideal spot. He measured the distance to the next big tree and girded himself. Since it was unlikely the grizzled frontiersman would come to him, he had to take the fight to Weasel.

A stealthy tread gave Fargo a fraction of a second's warning that someone was sneaking up on him. He ducked and whirled as tapered steel cleaved the space his neck had just occupied. Trevane snarled and swung again, slicing at the wrist to Fargo's gun hand. The blow connected, but not with the razor edge, as Trevane had intended. The flat of the blade struck against bone, numbing Fargo's hand. The Colt slipped from his grasp as he skipped to the left to evade a third slash.

"You're mine!" Trevane gloated, wagging the tip of his sword. "I'll whittle you down piece by piece."

Suddenly, Fargo realized that he was in the open, his back to the pines that concealed Weasel. He feinted to the left, then reversed himself and bounded right. The ruse worked. The dandy speared the sword to the left. At the same moment, the woods thundered to the blast of Weasel's Sharps. The slug that would have caught Fargo in the back smashed into Trevane's chest instead, flinging him to the turf with his limbs disjointed and his mouth agape.

Diving, Fargo retrieved his Colt. He had glimpsed the muzzle flash of the Sharps. It came from midway up a tall pine, where an indistinct ebony silhouette squatted on a limb. Aiming at the center of the crouched shape, Fargo squeezed off two shots, emptying his pistol.

A strangled outcry heralded the crash of limbs as the figure plummeted. It bounced off the bole, dropped onto the lowest branch with a sharp crack of breaking bones, then flopped to earth.

Fargo barged through the weeds to the pines, replacing one of the spent cartridges as he ran. He was ready to finish the frontiersman off, but a third shot was not needed.

Weasel's neckbone had been shattered. His cheek rested on his shoulder, his tongue protruded.

Two down, one to go, Fargo told himself. He reached for his cartridge belt to finish reloading, and it was then that a steam engine slammed into his back. Or so it felt, as he was thrown against the pine, the world around him bursting in a shower of fiery pinpoints of light. Hands made of iron clamped onto his neck. Fingers as thick as cables squeezed, choking off his air.

"You're all mine!" Darnell rasped.

Fargo found himself on his knees, his senses reeling. He tried to pry Darnell's fingers off, but they would not budge.

He battered Darnell's forearms. He thrashed from side to side. Nothing worked. Little by little, Darnell was strangling the life from him. His hand fell to his right boot, to the hilt of the toothpick.

"Die!" Darnell raged.

Twisting, Fargo thrust blindly upward. He felt the blade penetrate, felt blood gush over his hand. Again he stabbed, and a third time. The pressure on his neck relaxed; the fingers fell away. Spinning, Fargo watched Darnell totter, grasping at limbs for support.

One snapped, pitching Darnell onto his face. Propping a hand, he tried to stand. He couldn't. "I'll be damned," he said. And just like that, Tharon Lucien Darnell, the richest man in three states, the tyrant who had clawed and bullied and murdered his way to the top of a vast financial empire, the brute who had delighted in battering and beating his own wife and daughter, faded into oblivion.

"You did it, Skye."

Fargo turned. Rosalie and Mandy were staring at the body. Bethany was behind them. "Don't you ever listen when someone tells you to stay put?" he asked.

"It's just a flesh wound," Rosalie said. "I feel fine." Hugging Amanda, she smiled for the first time since she had met Fargo. "Really, really fine."

*1860, New Mexico Territory,
where hatred and greed
spawned a killing ground . . .*

Gunshots blasted crisp and clear in the dry New Mexico air. Five loud ones in swift succession, followed by two more, fainter. Skye Fargo had no trouble pinpointing the direction they came from. Hardly had the sounds faded than the big man tapped his spurs against the Ovaro and galloped toward a rise to the southeast.

The Trailsman was in hostile country, on temporary dispatch duty for the Army. There were Apaches to watch out for. Utes as well. Not to mention roving bands of cutthroats who preyed in growing numbers on unwary travelers, renegades and outcasts who had given New Mexico a reputation as not being fit for greenhorns.

Not that anyone would ever brand Skye Fargo a tenderfoot. Tall, broad-shouldered, and powerfully built, he was the sort of man others tended to shy from. One look into his piercing lake-blue eyes was enough to convince most people that riling him would have the same result as riling a grizzly.

Hat brim pulled low against the blistering sun, Fargo reined up just below the crest. Rising in the stirrups, he scanned the arid terrain beyond.

Excerpt from PECOS DEATH

New Mexico in July was an oven. Shimmering waves of heat rippled from the baked earth. Mesquite, yucca, and purple sage grew where little else could, the sage adding a dash of color to the otherwise bleak landscape. Of wildlife there was no sign, with the lone exception of a large hawk lazily circling.

Fargo ventured higher, taking the risk of exposing himself in the hope of locating the source of the gunfire. Almost immediately, from a canyon on his right, echoed another ragged volley. It was answered by two single shots spaced seconds apart. From the sound of things, someone with a pistol was up against three or four rifles.

Few lone riders would bother to investigate. It was simply too risky a proposition. On the frontier any hombre who stuck his nose in where it did not belong ran the risk of having his fool head shot off. For all Fargo knew, Apaches were involved, and no one in his right mind cared to tangle with the Mescaleros or Jicarillas.

Yet Fargo did not hesitate. Someone might need help, and he was the only help handy. Flicking his reins, he trotted to the canyon north. Along the way he slid his shiny Henry rifle from its scabbard. Working the lever, he fed a .44 cartridge into the chamber.

Ground chewed up by hoofprints told part of the story. A lone rider had been chased into the canyon by four others. Who they were, and what they were doing so far from civilization, was a mystery Fargo aimed to solve by dismounting and warily cat-footing forward.

Rifles thundered, the retorts rumbling off the high stone walls like so much thunder. Somewhere a horse whinnied in pain. The pistol answered the rifles, only to be drowned out by another blistering round of leaden fury.

Around the next bend the clash raged. Fargo crept to the edge, then peeked out. Acrid smoke hung thick and heavy, wafting above a large boulder that shielded four riflemen.

Their backs were to him. Two were armed with Henrys, one with a Sharps, the last held a Volcanic Arms carbine.

A grungy character whose red bandanna was stained with grime motioned for the others to stop firing. Cupping a hand to his mouth, he hollered, "Cambridge, this is Grifter! Make it easy on yourself! Toss those saddlebags out where we can get 'em, and we'll take 'em and skedaddle. What do you say?"

No one answered.

"Use your head, damn it!" the grimy man said. "Is it worth your life? You don't owe Stockwell anything."

Still, Cambridge did not respond.

"I'm tryin' to be reasonable," Grifter huffed. "But if this is how you want it, fine by me. We can wait you out, you know. We have plenty of water. But you can't get to your canteen without us blowin' your head off." He paused to let that bit of information sink in. "So what will it be? Do you hand it over or not?"

Cambridge answered with a shot that whined off the boulder. Flying rock slivers forced Grifter and his friends to duck. Swearing luridly, Grifter gave the order to fire and all four men cut loose, their rifles hammering in deafening cadence. They stopped only when they emptied their weapons.

Fargo had no idea what the fight was about, or who was in the right. But he had taken an instinctive dislike to Grifter. The man was a human sidewinder if ever there was one. And Grifter's companions were cut from the same coarse cloth. He was about to show himself when a strident nicker reminded him of the stricken horse.

A weasel in baggy pants and a floppy hat moved to the end of the boulder, fed a cartridge into his Sharps, and took deliberate aim. "I hate for any critter to suffer," he commented.

Grifter chortled. "Let the nag raise a fuss, Zeke. Maybe it'll convince that stubborn yack to do what's best."

"It ain't right to let anything die slow and painful," Zeke insisted. "My pa taught me that when I was still a sprout."

"Lordy!" Grifter said, nudging one of the others. "Hear that, Hardwick? We got us a good Samaritan here! Next thing you know, he'll climb up on this boulder and give us a sermon about how we have to mend our wicked ways."

Hardwick and the fourth man snickered. Zeke shifted from one foot to the other and said sullenly, "I won't do no such thing, neither. All I'm sayin' is—"

"I know what you're sayin'!" Grifter unexpectedly exploded, lunging and seizing Zeke by the front of his homespun shirt. "The problem is that you're talkin' when you should be listenin'! I want the stinkin' horse left to rot. You got that?"

Zeke had blanched. Swallowing hard, he bobbed his pointed chin. "Sure, Tom. Sure. Don't get yourself in a huff. I know better than to buck you."

"You'd better," Grifter said, shoving the smaller man against the boulder. "I don't like being sassed. Ever."

The man called Hardwick fished cartridges from a shirt pocket. Bearded and unkempt, he had a belly that would do justice to a hog. "Do you really aim to sit here in this hot sun and wait Cambridge out?"

"Of course not," Grifter said. "As soon as it's dark, the four of us will close in. We should be able to sneak right up on her."

Fargo stiffened. Had he heard correctly? Her? Leveling the Henry, he inched around the corner. The four men were so busy reloading that they had no inkling of his presence. Less than ten feet from them, he planted both boots and declared, "Drop the rifles, gents."

All four spun. Hardwick and the fourth man froze. Zeke's mouth worked like that of a carp out of water, his eyelids fluttering like butterfly wings. Grifter started to bring up his rifle, stopping only when the muzzle of Fargo's Henry swung toward his stomach.

"Didn't you hear me? Set the hardware down, boys. Real slow."

Reluctantly, baffled anger contorting his features, Grifter complied. It was the cue for the others to do likewise. Zeke promptly elevated his hands. Hardwick, though, held his left arm cocked as if he were tempted to make a stab for his Remington revolver.

"If you reckon you're faster than a bullet, go ahead," Fargo said, smirking. "If not, I'd advise all of you to shuck the belt guns."

Livid with fury, Grifter unbuckled his gun belt and lowered it to the ground. "I don't like it when others butt into my affairs," he growled.

Fargo was watching Hardwick. The heavyset cutthroat was taking his sweet time unbuckling. He wasn't fooling anyone. Hardwick was itching to turn the tables, and was hoping Fargo would lower his guard for just a second.

"What's your stake in this, mister?" Grifter asked, eyes glittering like those of a rabid wolf eager to pounce. "Who the hell are you, anyway?"

Ignoring him, Fargo angled toward them. He gazed deeper into the canyon as if trying to spot the person they had been shooting at. Out of the corner of his eye he saw Hardwick begin to ease the gun belt down. The gunman was holding it in such a way that the holster was close to his stomach, and close to his right hand.

Suddenly Hardwick clawed at the Remington. He was fast, all right, but not fast enough. Not by a long shot. Fargo took two quick bounds and slammed the Henry's stock against the man's temple, felling Hardwick like a pole ox.

Zeke and the fourth owlhoot backed off, not wanting any part of him. But Grifter lunged, his brawny arms outstretched, sadistic glee curling his thin lips. He thought that he had Fargo dead to rights. He was wrong.

Shifting, the Trailsman rammed the barrel into Grifter's gut. Grifter doubled over, flushing scarlet, his lungs expelling a breath in a loud *whoosh*. Clutching his abdomen, he tottered, spittle flecking his chin.

"How about you two?" Fargo said to Zeke and the fourth man. Both vigorously shook their heads, Zeke's eyelids fluttering more madly than before.

Grifter did not know when he was well off. Jabbing a finger, he snarled, "No one does that to me and gets away with it! No one! By the time I'm through, you'll beg me to put you out of your misery, you rotten son of a—"

The cutthroat got no further. Fargo swung the Henry in a tight arc, the stock catching Grifter squarely on the cheek and splitting it like an overripe melon. Grifter staggered, blood spurting. A roar of white-hot rage spewed from his throat. Forgetting himself, the big ruffian lunged again. This time Fargo brought the stock up and around, smashing it against Grifter's jaw. Teeth crunched. Grifter's head was jolted backward, and he rocked on his heels. Then, like melting wax, the hothead oozed to the earth, unconscious.

"Lordy!" Zeke said. "I ain't ever seen anybody get the better of Tom before."

"That makes two of us," said the fourth man, awed.

Fargo backed off, the Henry steady at his side. "When he comes around, tell him he's welcome to look me up any time he wants." Fargo nodded to the west, at a cluster of boulders. Four mounts waited there. "Tote your friends over and throw them on their horses."

Zeke meekly complied. "Whatever you say, friend. Just don't do to me what you did to Tom. I ain't got all that many teeth left as it is." To demonstrate, he opened his mouth wide, revealing a gap where several of his lower front ones had been. Those on the top were yellow or dark with rot. "It's gettin' so I'll be gummin' my food before I'm fifty."

Zeke took hold of Grifter's wrists, the other man picked up the legs, and working together, they shuffled toward their animals, going from boulder to boulder in order not to expose themselves to the woman up the canyon. After draping their burden over a dun, they returned for Hardwick.

"Damn," Zeke groused as he puffed along like a steam engine. "I wish to blazes this varmint would quit eatin' so much. Any heavier, I'd pull a groin muscle."

Hoisting Hardwick onto his sorrel proved to be a challenge. Zeke and the fourth gunman strained and heaved and sputtered, Zeke sagging against the horse in relief when they finally succeeded. "Jehosophat! It's a wonder he can find britches that fit. I'd be downright embarrassed to go through life lookin' like one of those big blue fish with holes in the tops of their heads."

"They're called whales," Fargo said.

"That's them," Zeke confirmed. "Saw a couple once, when I was in California. They were blowin' and rollin' and havin' a grand old time." The beanpole scratched himself. "Almost made me wish I was one. I'll bet they don't have a care in the world."

Fargo pegged Zeke as one of those who jabbered worse than chipmunks. "Climb on and head out," he directed.

"What about our shooting irons and our rifles?" asked the last member of the foursome.

Zeke nodded. "Surely you ain't fixin' to have us wander around unarmed? Hell, ain't you heard that Mescaleros have been seen hereabouts recently? We'll lose our hides."

"I'll leave your guns right where they are," Fargo proposed. "In about an hour you can come back and claim them." It was the best he could do. Allowing them to take their hardware invited a shot in the back once Grifter and Hardwick revived. Wagging the Henry, he shooed them on their way. Zeke, leading Grifter's mount, grinned and waved as if they were the best of friends.

Fargo did not budge until they were well out of the canyon and bearing to the south. Then, pivoting, he jogged to the huge boulder. Leaning against it, he called out, "Lady! I'm a friend. Did you hear those horses leave? The men who were giving you a hard time are gone. It's safe to come out."

The woman did not reply. Fargo repeated himself, adding, "I'm not out to hurt you. I'm riding dispatch for the Army and just happened by."

Silence reigned. Fargo wondered if maybe the woman had been hit and was lying out there somewhere, bleeding to death. Sidling to where he could see up the canyon, he spied a horse on its side forty yards away. A spreading crimson pool explained why. Grifter and his friends must have shot it out from under her.

"Ma'am? Can you hear me?" Fargo tried one more time.

"I hear you just fine," said a low, sultry voice to his rear. "Now be so kind as to put down that rifle and raise your arms."

"But I'm not out to—" Fargo began, turning, and was riveted to the spot by the sharp retort of a pistol and the *spang* of a slug off the boulder by his shoulder. He did as she had requested.

"You learn quick," the woman said. "Who are you?" she asked suspiciously. "How can you claim to be a soldier when you're not wearing a uniform?"

"I never claimed I was *in* the Army," Fargo clarified. "I like my freedom too much. I could never stand still for always having someone tell me what to do." As he spoke, he slowly faced her. He did not know what he expected, but certainly not to find a stunning blonde whose alluring eyes were a shade richer blue than his own. She was dressed in scuffed boots, baggy pants, and a loose shirt that hid the contours of her body. A battered black hat crowned her golden mane. Around her slender waist was strapped a cartridge belt. In her right hand, fixed on his chest, was a cocked Smith & Wesson.

"What's your handle?" the beauty demanded.

The Trailsman told her. "I'm carrying a dispatch to Cantonment Burgwin." The post had been built eight years ago by the 1st U.S. Dragoons to protect the Taos Valley from Apaches and Utes. Never officially designated a fort, it was due to close in a few weeks. "Your name is Cambridge?" he prodded.

"Ivy Cambridge," the blonde confirmed. "I was on my way to Sumner's Trading Post when Grifter and his pack of polecats bushwhacked me. Damn them all to hell."

"What were they after?" Fargo asked.

Ivy shrugged. "What do you think?" she said. "I'm a female, aren't I?"

There was no denying that. Despite the bulky clothes, she had a sensual allure that turned Fargo's thoughts to wondering how she would look in clothes that fit. Put her in a tight dress and spruce up her hair and she would be a whole new woman. But Fargo doubted that her being female had anything to do with why she was waylaid. Still, if that was what she wanted him to believe, so be it.

"I'd be obliged if we could ride double as far as Cantonment Burgwin," Ivy said. "I can pick up a new horse there and ride on back to fetch my saddle and bedroll. What do you say?"

"I'll go you one better," Fargo said. "We'll rig up a travois to carry your gear."

"A what?"

"You'll see." Fargo pointed at the Smith & Wesson. "So can I move? Or do you intend to keep me covered all the way to the post?"

Cambridge twirled the revolver into her holster with a

flourish that would have done any savvy gunhand proud. Patting the smooth butt, she said, "Just remember. I know how to use this. Any shenanigans, and I'll give you some lead pills for what ails you."

Fargo laughed, sincerely liking her brash nature. Women on the frontier were a generally tougher lot than their city-bred sisters. They had to be, what with hostiles and wild beasts and white man who were little better than beasts themselves. Country gals did not tolerate nonsense. And any man who tried to take advantage was asking to eat his own teeth. "Don't fret," he assured her. "I know how to behave."

"Do you indeed?" Ivy said skeptically. "If so, you're one of a rare breed, Mr. Fargo. Most men can't keep their hands off a pretty woman if their lives depend on it." She paused, gazing in the direction the four hardcases had taken. "Tom Grifter is a prime example. The man thinks God gave him the right to ride roughshod over any female he wants."

"That sounds like experience talking," Fargo noted.

The blonde scowled and changed the subject. "So what in the world is a travois, anyhow? That's a new one on me."

Obviously, she had never lived among the Plains tribes, or among the Indians who called the northern Rockies their home. Travois were commonly used to transport lodges, parfleches, and other belongings.

Fargo related as much as he scoured their vicinity for two long limbs. Trees, though, were few and far between. He had to settle for four short branches chopped off a stunted pine. Rope sufficed to lash them into pairs long enough to serve as the frame for the platform. Trimming enough smaller limbs to fashion the platform at one end of the makeshift poles took about a half hour.

The sun was high in the sky when Fargo tied the opposite ends of the poles to the Ovaro's saddle. Ivy's saddle and bedroll were secured on the travois. Her saddlebags she insisted on slinging over a shoulder.

They were set to leave. Stepping to the dead mare, Ivy regarded the animal in quiet respect for a bit, then gave it the highest compliment any mount could receive. "She never gave me cause to complain. I feel wrong, leaving her for the scavengers like this."

Fargo tilted his head skyward. Already a half dozen buzzards were circling. Soon there would be three times as many. By nightfall coyotes would show up, or maybe a mountain lion would catch wind of the blood and investigate. In three days there would be little left of the mare except bones and a pool of dry blood. "Let's get going while we have some daylight left," he said.

Ivy had to climb on first, carefully sliding her legs over the poles and making herself as comfortable as she could. Fargo forked leather and clucked to the pinto. Neither of them had a word to say until they came to a steep gully Fargo could not go around. As they angled down the slope, the stallion gave a lurch. Ivy was thrown against Fargo's back, her bosom mashing against his shoulder blades.

"Sorry," she bleated.

"No need to be," Fargo said. "You'd better hold on. I want to put as many miles behind us as I can." He had planned on reaching the post by the middle of the next morning. Now it would be late in the afternoon, or early evening. Which meant the two of them had to spend the night together.

Not that Fargo indulged in any frisky notions. Ivy Cambridge kept one hand on her six-shooter at all times. She rode easily, relaxed, at home on horseback, indicating she had spent a lot of time in the saddle. A faint hint of perfume mingled with her natural earthy scent to tingle Fargo's nostrils. The warm feel of her body on his back and the caress of her breath on his neck was enough to prickle his skin from head to toe.

Over an hour went by without Ivy Cambridge saying a word. Fargo did not pester her with questions about where she was from or what she was doing in that neck of the woods. It was none of his business. Prying was a bad habit of those who were too full of themselves for their own good.

Besides, Fargo was accustomed to being quiet. Traveling alone for days or even weeks at a time, as he often did, gave a person a whole new appreciation for golden silence.

Ivy cleared her throat. "I never did thank you for coming to my rescue back yonder. If you hadn't shown up when you did, those boys might have made wolf meat of me."

"Maybe," Fargo said. "But I'd bet my poke that you would have taken a few of them with you."

Her laughter rippled like the bubbling of a frosty mountain stream. "You're a shrewd judge of character, Mr. Fargo. Yes, I would do my damnedest to make those bastards pay. I'd like to leave this old world the same way I came into it, kicking and screaming."

"You're shy of them now," Fargo reminded her. "If they have any brains at all, they won't badger you again."

"You wouldn't say that if you knew Grifter as well as I do."

Just then, almost as if on cue, the crack of a rifle shattered the stillness. Twisting, Fargo saw the four cutthroats bearing down at a gallop, rifles pressed to their shoulders. In the center was Tom Grifter, his battered and swollen face lit by hellish savagery.

"We've got them now, boys! Cut them down, horse and all!"

SIGNET

THE WILD FRONTIER

☐ **JUSTIS COLT by Don Bendell.** The Colt Family Saga continues, with the danger, passion, and adventure of the American West. When Texas Ranger Justis Colt is ambushed by a gang of murderers, a mysterious stranger, Tora, saves his life. But now the motley crew of outlaws demand revenge and kill Tora's wife and two sons. Vengeance becomes a double-edged sword as Colt and Tora face the challenge of hunting down the killers.
(182421—$4.99)

☐ **THE KILLING SEASON by Ralph Compton.** It was the 1870s—and the West was at its wildest. One man rode like a legend of death on this untamed frontier. His name was Nathan Stone, and he has learned to kill on the vengeance trail. He would have stopped after settling the score with his parents' savage slayers. But when you are the greatest gunfighter of all, there is no peace or resting place. . .
(187873—$5.99)

☐ **THE HOMESMAN by Glendon Swarthout.** Briggs was an army deserter and claim jumper who was as low as a man could get. Mary Bee Cuddy was a spinster homesteader who acted like she was as good as any man. Together they had to take back east four women who had gone out of their minds and out of control. "An epic journey across the plains . . . as good as novels get."—
Cleveland Plain Dealer (190319—$5.99)

*Prices slightly higher in Canada

Buy them at your local bookstore or use this convenient coupon for ordering.

PENGUIN USA
P.O. Box 999 — Dept. #17109
Bergenfield, New Jersey 07621

Please send me the books I have checked above.
I am enclosing $_____ (please add $2.00 to cover postage and handling). Send check or money order (no cash or C.O.D.'s) or charge by Mastercard or VISA (with a $15.00 minimum). Prices and numbers are subject to change without notice.

Card #_____ Exp. Date _____
Signature_____
Name_____
Address_____
City _____ State _____ Zip Code _____

For faster service when ordering by credit card call **1-800-253-6476**

Allow a minimum of 4-6 weeks for delivery. This offer is subject to change without notice.